Red Pepper's Patients

Grace S. Richmond

TUTIS Digital Publishing Pvt Ltd

ISBN 978-81-8456-432-7

Red Pepper's Patients

This impression 2007

Published by

TUTIS Digital Publishing Pvt Ltd.

26 Ramasamy Street

T. Nagar, Chennai 600 017

CONTENTS

CHAPTER I

An Intelligent Prescription

The man in the silk-lined, London-made overcoat, holding his hat firmly on his head lest the January wind send its expensive perfection into the gutter, paused to ask his way of the man with no overcoat, his hands shoved into his ragged pockets, his shapeless headgear crowded down over his eyes, red and bleary with the piercing wind.

"Burns?" repeated the second man to the question of the first. "Doc Burns? Sure! Next house beyond the corner—the brick one." He turned to point. "Tell it by the rigs hitched. It's his office hours. You'll do some waitin', tell ye that."

The questioner smiled—a slightly superior smile. "Thank you," he said, and passed on. He arrived at the corner and paused briefly, considering the row of vehicles in front of the old, low-lying brick house with its comfortable, white-pillared porches. The row was indeed a formidable one and suggested many waiting people within the house. But after an instant's hesitation he turned up the gravel path toward the wing of the house upon whose door could be seen the lettering of an inconspicuous sign. As he came near he made out that the sign read "R.P. Burns, M.D.," and that the table of office hours below set forth that the present hour was one of those designated.

"I'll get a line on your practice, Red," said the stranger to himself, and laid hand upon the doorbell. "Incidentally, perhaps, I'll get a line on why you stick to a small suburban town like this when you might be in the thick of things. A fellow whom I've twice met in Vienna, too. I can't understand it."

A fair-haired young woman in a white uniform and cap admitted the newcomer and pointed him to the one chair left unoccupied in the large and crowded waiting-room. It was a pleasant room, in a well-worn sort of way, and the blazing wood fire in a sturdy fireplace, the rows of dull-toned books cramming a solid phalanx of bookcases, and a number of interesting old prints on the walls gave it, as the stranger, lifting critical eyes, was obliged to admit to himself, a curious air of dignity in spite of the mingled atmosphere of drugs and patients which assailed his fastidious nostrils. As for the patients themselves, since they were all about him, he could hardly do less than observe them, although he helped himself to a late magazine from a well-filled table at his side and mechanically turned its pages.

The first to claim his attention was a little girl at his elbow. She could hardly fail to catch his eye, she was so conspicuous with bandages. One eye, one cheek, the whole of her neck, and both her hands were swathed in white, but the other cheek was rosy, and the uncovered eye twinkled bravely as she smiled at the stranger. "I was burned," she said proudly.

"I see," returned the stranger, speaking very low, for he was conscious that the entire roomful of people was listening. "And you are getting better?"

"Oh, yes!" exulted the child. "Doctor's making me have new skin. He gets me more new skin every day. I didn't have any at all. It was all burned off."

"That's very good of him," murmured the stranger.

"He's awful good," said the child, "when he isn't cross. He isn't ever cross to me, Doctor isn't."

There was a general murmur of amusement in the room, and another child, not far away, laughed aloud. The stranger furtively scrutinized the other patients one by one, lifting apparently casual glances from behind his magazine. Several, presumably the owners of the vehicles outside, were of the typical village type, but there were others more sophisticated, and several who were palpably persons of wealth. One late comer was admitted who left a luxuriously appointed motor across the street, and brought in with her an atmosphere of costly furs and violets and fresh air.

"Certainly a mixed crowd," said the stranger to himself behind his magazine; "but not so different, after all, from most doctors' waiting-room crowds. I might send in a card, but, if I remember Red, it wouldn't get me anything—and this is rather interesting anyhow. I'll wait."

He waited, for he wished the waiting room to be clear when he should approach that busy consulting room beyond. Meanwhile, people came and went. The door into the inner room would swing open, a patient would emerge, a curt but pleasant "Good-bye" in a deep voice following him or her out, and the fair-haired nurse, who sat at a desk near the door or came out of the consulting room with the patient, would summon the next. The lady of the furs and violets sent in her card, but, as the stranger had anticipated in his own case, it procured her no more than an assurance from the nurse that Doctor Burns would see her in due course. Since he wanted the coast clear the stranger, when at last his turn arrived, politely waived his rights, sent the furs and violets in before him, and sat alone with the nurse in the cleared waiting room.

A comparatively short period of time elapsed before the consulting-room door opened once more. But it closed again—

almost—and a few words reached the outer room.

"Oh, but you're hard—hard, Doctor Burns! I simply can't do it," said a plaintive voice.

"Then don't expect me to accomplish anything. It's up to you—absolutely," replied a brusque voice, which then softened slightly as it added: "Cheer up. You can, you know. Good-bye."

The patient came out, her lips set, her eyes lowered, and left the office as if she wanted nothing so much as to get away. The nurse rose and began to say that Doctor Burns would now see his one remaining caller, but at that moment Doctor Burns himself appeared in the doorway, glanced at the stranger, who had risen, smiling—and the need for an intermediary between physician and patient vanished before the onslaught of the physician himself.

"My word! Gardner Coolidge! Well, well—if this isn't the greatest thing on earth. My dear fellow!"

The stranger, no longer a stranger, with

his hand being wrung like that, with his eyes being looked into by a pair of glowing hazel eyes beneath a heavy thatch of well-remembered coppery hair, returned this demonstration of affection with equal fervour.

"I've been sitting in your stuffy waiting room, Red, till the entire population of this town should tell you its aches, just for the pleasure of seeing you with the professional manner off."

Burns threw back his head and laughed, with a gesture as of flinging something aside. "It's off then, Cooly—if I have one. I didn't know I had. How are you? Man, but it's good to see you! Come along out of this into a place that's not stuffy. Where's your bag? You didn't leave it anywhere?"

"I can't stay, Red—really I can't. Not this time. I must go to-night. And I came to consult you professionally—so let's get that over first."

"Of course. Just let me speak a word to the authorities. You'll at least be here for dinner? Step into the next room, Cooly. On your way let me present you to my assistant, Miss Mathewson, whom I couldn't do without. Mr. Coolidge, Miss Mathewson."

Gardner Coolidge bowed to the office nurse, whom he had already classified as a very attractively superior person and well worth a good salary; then went on into the consulting room, where an open window had freshened the small place beyond any possibility of its being called stuffy. As he closed the window with a shiver and looked about him, glancing into the white-tiled surgery beyond; he recognized the fact that, though he might be in the workshop of a village practitioner, it was a workshop which did not lack the tools of the workman thoroughly abreast of the times.

Burns came back, his face bright with pleasure in the unexpected appearance of his friend. He stood looking across the small room at Coolidge, as if he could get a better view of the whole man at a little distance. The two men were a decided contrast to each other. Redfield Pepper Burns, known to all his intimates, and to many more who would not have ventured to call him by that title, as "Red Pepper Burns," on account of the combination of red head, quick temper, and wit which were his most distinguishing characteristics of body and mind, was a stalwart fellow whose weight was effectually kept down by his activity. His white linen office jacket was filled by powerful shoulders, and the perfectly kept hands of the surgeon gave evidence, as such hands do, of their delicacy of touch, in the very way in which Burns closed the door behind him.

Gardner Coolidge was of a different type altogether. As tall as Burns, he looked taller because of his slender figure and the distinctive outlines of his careful dress. His face was dark and rather thin, showing sensitive lines about the eyes and mouth, and a tendency to melancholy in the eyes themselves, even when lighted by a smile, as now. He was manifestly the man of worldly experience, with fastidious tastes, and presumably one who did not accept the rest of mankind as comrades until proved and chosen.

"So it's my services you want?" questioned Burns. "If that's the case, then it's here you sit."

"Face to the light, of course," objected Coolidge with a grimace. "I wonder if you doctors know what a moral advantage as well as a physical one that gives you."

"Of course. The moral advantage is the one we need most. Anybody can see when a skin is jaundiced; but only by virtue of that moral standpoint can we detect the soul out of order. And that's the matter with you, Cooly."

"What!" Coolidge looked startled. "I knew you were a man who jumped to conclusions in the old days—"

"And acted on them, too," admitted Burns. "I should say I did. And got myself into many a scrape thereby, of course. Well, I jump to conclusions now, in just the same way, only perhaps with a bit more understanding of the ground I jump on. However, tell me your symptoms in orthodox style, please, then we'll have them out of the way."

Coolidge related them somewhat reluctantly because, as he went on, he was conscious that they did not appear to be of as great importance as this visit to a physician seemed to indicate he thought them. The most impressive was the fact that he was unable to get a thoroughly good night's sleep except when physically exhausted, which in his present manner of life he seldom was. When he had finished and looked around—he had been gazing out of the window—he found himself, as he had known he should, under the intent scrutiny of the eyes he was facing.

"What did the last man give you for this insomnia?" was the abrupt question.

"How do you know I have been to a succession of men?" demanded Coolidge with a touch of evident irritation.

"Because you come to me. We don't look up old friends in the profession until the strangers fail us," was the quick reply.

"More hasty conclusions. Still, I'll have to admit that I let our family physician look me over, and that he suggested my seeing a nerve man—Allbright. He has rather a name, I believe?"

"Sure thing. What did he recommend?"

"A long sea voyage. I took it—having nothing else to do—and slept a bit better while I was away. The minute I got back it was the old story."

"Nothing on your mind, I suppose?" suggested Burns.

"I supposed you'd ask me that stock question. Why shouldn't there be something on my mind? Is there anybody whose mind is free from a weight of some sort?" demanded Gardner Coolidge. His thin face flushed a little.

"Nobody," admitted Burns promptly. "The question is whether the weight on yours is one that's got to stay there or whether you may be rid of it. Would you care to tell me anything about it? I'm a pretty old friend, you know."

Coolidge was silent for a full minute, then he spoke with evident reluctance: "It won't do a particle of good to tell, but I suppose, if I consult you, you have a right to know the facts. My wife—has gone back to her father."

"On a visit?" Burns inquired.

Coolidge stared at him. "That's like you,

Red," he said, irritation in his voice again. "What's the use of being brutal?"

"Has she been gone long enough for people to think it's anything more than a visit?"

"I suppose not. She's been gone two months. Her home is in California."

"Then she can be gone three without anybody's thinking trouble. By the end of that third month you can bring her home," said Burns comfortably. He leaned back in his swivel-chair, and stared hard at the ceiling.

Coolidge made an exclamation of displeasure and got to his feet. "If you don't care to take me seriously—" he began.

"I don't take any man seriously who I know cared as much for his wife when he married her as you did for Miss Carrington—and whose wife was as much in love with him as she was with you—when he comes to me and talks about her having gone on a visit to her father. Visits are good things; they make people appreciate each other."

"You don't—or won't—understand." Coolidge evidently strove hard to keep himself quiet. "We have come to a definite understanding that we can't—get on together. She's not coming back. And I don't want her to."

Burns lowered his gaze from the ceiling to his friend's face, and the glance he now gave him was piercing. "Say that last again," he demanded.

"I have some pride," replied the other haughtily, but his eyes would not meet Burns's.

"So I see. Pride is a good thing. So is love. Tell me you don't love her and I'll—No, don't tell me that. I don't want to hear you perjure yourself. And I shouldn't believe you. You may as well own up"—his voice was gentle now—"that you're suffering—and not only with hurt pride." There was silence for a little. Then Burns began again, in a very low and quiet tone: "Have you anything against her, Cooly?"

The man before him, who was still standing, turned upon him. "How can you ask me such a question?" he said fiercely.

"It's a question that has to be asked, just to get it out of the way. Has she anything against you?"

"For heaven's sake—no! You know us both."

"I thought I did. Diagnosis, you know, is a series of eliminations. And now I can eliminate pretty nearly everything from this case except a certain phrase you used a few minutes ago. I'm inclined to think it's the cause of the trouble." Coolidge looked his inquiry. "'*Having nothing else to do.*'"

Coolidge shook his head. "You're mistaken there. I have plenty to do."

"But nothing you couldn't be spared from—unless things have changed since the days when we all envied you. You're still writing your name on the backs of dividend drafts, I suppose?"

"Red, you are something of a brute," said Coolidge, biting his lip. But he had taken the chair again.

"I know," admitted Red Pepper Burns. "I don't really mean to be, but the only way I can find out the things I need to know is to ask straight questions. I never could stand circumlocution. If you want that, Cooly; if you want what are called 'tactful' methods, you'll have to go to some other man. What I mean by asking you that one is to prove to you that though you may have something to do, you have no job to work at. As it happens you haven't even what most other rich men have, the trouble of looking after your income—and as long as your father lives you won't have it. I understand that; he won't let you. But there's a man with a job—your father. And he likes it so well he won't share it with you. It isn't the money he values, it's the job. And collecting books or curios or coins can never be made to take the place of good, downright hard work."

"That may be all true," acknowledged Coolidge, "but it has nothing to do with my present trouble. My leisure was not what—" He paused, as if he could not bear to discuss the subject of his marital unhappiness.

The telephone bell in the outer office rang sharply. An instant later Miss Mathewson knocked, and gave a message to Burns. He read it, nodded, said "Right away," and turned back to his friend.

"I have to leave you for a bit," he said. "Come in and meet my wife and one of the kiddies. The other's away just now. I'll be back in time for dinner. Meanwhile, we'll let the finish of this talk wait over for an hour or two. I want to think about it."

He exchanged his white linen office-jacket for a street coat, splashing about with soap and water just out of sight for a little while before he did so, and reappeared looking as if he had washed away the fatigue of his afternoon's work with the physical process. He led Gardner Coolidge out of the offices into a wide separating hall, and the moment the door closed behind him the visitor felt as if he had entered a different world.

Could this part of the house, he thought, as Burns ushered him into the living room on the other side of the hall and left him there while he went to seek his wife, possibly be contained within the old brick walls of the exterior? He had not dreamed of finding such refinement of beauty and charm in connection with the office of the village doctor. In half a dozen glances to right and left Gardner Coolidge, experienced in appraising the belongings of the rich and travelled of superior taste and breeding, admitted to himself that the genius of the place must be such a woman as he would not have imagined Redfield Pepper Burns able to marry.

He had not long to wait for the confirmation of his insight. Burns shortly returned, a two-year-old boy on his shoulder, his wife following, drawn along by the child's hand. Coolidge looked, and liked that which he saw. And he understood, with one glance into the dark eyes which met his, one look at the firm sweetness of the lovely mouth, that the heart of the husband must safely trust in this woman.

Burns went away at once, leaving Coolidge in the company of Ellen, and the guest, eager though he was for the professional advice he had come to seek, could not regret the necessity which gave him this hour with a woman who seemed to him very unusual. Charm she possessed in full measure, beauty in no less, but neither of these terms nor both together could wholly describe Ellen Burns. There was something about her which seemed to glow, so that he soon felt that her presence in the quietly rich and restful living room completed its furnishing, and that once having seen her there the place could never be quite at its best without her.

Burns came back, and the three went out to dinner. The small boy, a handsome, auburn-haired, brown-eyed composite of his parents, had been sent away, the embraces of both father and mother consoling him for his banishment to the arms of a coloured mammy. Coolidge thoroughly enjoyed the simple but appetizing dinner, of the sort he had known he should have as soon as he had met the mistress of the house. And after it he was borne away by Burns to the office.

"I have to go out again at once," the physician announced. "I'm going to take you with me. I suppose you have a distaste for the sight of illness, but that doesn't matter seriously. I want you to see this patient of mine."

"Thank you, but I don't believe that's necessary," responded Coolidge with a frown. "If Mrs. Burns is too busy to keep me company I'll sit here and read while you're out."

"No, you won't. If you consult a man you're bound to take his prescriptions. I'm telling you frankly, for you'd see through me if I pretended to take you out for a walk and then pulled you into a house. Be a sport, Cooly."

"Very well," replied the other man, suppressing his irritation. He was almost, but not quite, wishing he had not yielded to the unexplainable impulse which had brought him here to see a man who, as he should have known from past experience in college days, was as sure to be eccentric in his methods of practising his profession as he had been in the conduct of his life as a student.

The two went out into the winter night together, Coolidge remarking that the call must be a brief one, for his train would leave in a little more than an hour.

"It'll be brief," Burns promised. "It's practically a friendly call only, for there's nothing more I can do for the patient—except to see him on his way."

Coolidge looked more than ever reluctant. "I hope he's not just leaving the world?"

"What if he were—would that frighten you? Don't be worried; he'll not go to-night."

Something in Burns's tone closed his companion's lips. Coolidge resented it, and at the same time he felt constrained to let the other have his way. And after all there proved to be nothing in the sight he presently found himself witnessing to shock the most delicate sensibilities.

It was a little house to which Burns conducted his friend and latest patient; it was a low-ceiled, homely room, warm with lamplight and comfortable with the accumulations of a lifetime carefully preserved. In the worn, old, red-cushioned armchair by a glowing stove sat an aged figure of a certain dignity and attractiveness in spite of the lines and hues plainly showing serious illness. The man was a man of education and experience, as was evident from his first words in response to Burns's greeting.

"It was kind of you to come again to-night, Doctor. I suspect you know how it shortens the nights to have this visit from you in the evening."

"Of course I know," Burns responded, his hand resting gently on the frail shoulder, his voice as tender as that of a son's to a father whom he knows he is not long to see.

There was a woman in the room, an old woman with a pathetic face and eyes like a mourning dog's as they rested on her husband. But her voice was cheerful and full of quiet courage as she answered Burns's questions. The pair received Gardner Coolidge as simply as if they were accustomed to meet strangers every day, spoke with him a little, and showed him the courtesy of genuine interest when he tried to entertain them with a brief account of an incident which had happened on his train that day. Altogether, there was nothing about the visit which he could have characterized as painful from the point of view of the layman who accompanies the physician to a room where it is clear that the great transition is soon to take place. And yet there was everything about it to make it painful—acutely painful—to any man whose discernment was naturally as keen as Coolidge's.

That the parting so near at hand was to be one between lovers of long standing could be read in every word and glance the two gave each other. That they were making the most of these last days was equally apparent, though not a word was said to suggest it. And that the man who was conducting them through the fast-diminishing time was dear to them as a son could have been read by the very blind.

"It's so good of you—so good of you, Doctor," they said again as Burns rose to go, and when he responded: "It's good to myself I am, my dears, when I come to look at you," the smiles they gave him and each other were very eloquent.

Outside there was silence between the two men for a little as they walked briskly along, then Coolidge said reluctantly: "Of course I should have a heart of stone if I were not touched by that scene—as you knew I would be."

"Yes, I knew," said Burns simply; and Coolidge saw him lift his hand and dash away a tear. "It gets me, twice a day regularly, just as if I hadn't seen it before. And when I go back and look at the woman I love I say to myself that I'll never let anything but the last enemy come between us if I have to crawl on my knees before her."

Suddenly Coolidge's throat contracted. His resentment against his friend was gone. Surely it was a wise physician who had given him that heartbreaking little scene to remember when he should be tempted to harden his heart against the woman he had chosen.

"Red," he said bye and bye, when the two were alone together for a few minutes again in the consulting room before he should leave for his train, "is that all the prescription you're going to give me—a trip to California? Suppose I'm not successful?"

Red Pepper Burns smiled, a curious little smile. "You've forgotten what I told you about the way my old man and woman made a home together,' and worked at their market gardening together, and read and studied together—did everything from first to last *together*. That's the whole force of the illustration, to my mind, Cooly. It's the standing shoulder to shoulder to face life that does the thing. Whatever plan you make for your after life, when you bring Alicia back with you—as you will; I know it—make it a plan which means partnership—if you have to build a cottage down on the edge of your estate and live alone there together. Alone till the children come to keep you company," he added with a sudden flashing smile.

Coolidge looked at him and shook his head. His face dropped back into melancholy. He opened his lips and closed them again. Red Pepper Burns opened his own lips—and closed them again. When he did speak it was to say, more gently than he had yet spoken:

"Old fellow, life isn't in ruins before you. Make up your mind to that. You'll sleep again, and laugh again—and cry again, too,—because life is like that, and you wouldn't want it any other way."

It was time for Coolidge to go, and the two men went in to permit the guest to take leave of Mrs. Burns. When they left the house Coolidge told his friend briefly what he thought of his friend's wife, and Burns smiled in the darkness as he heard.

"She affects most people that way," he answered with a proud little ring in his voice. But he did not go on to talk about her; that would have been brutal indeed in Coolidge's unhappy circumstances.

At the train Coolidge turned suddenly to his physician. "You haven't given me anything for my sleeplessness," he said.

"Think you must have a prescription?" Burns inquired, getting out his blank and pen.

"It will take some time for your advice to work out, if it ever does," Coolidge said. "Meanwhile, the more good sleep I get the fitter I shall be for the effort."

"True enough. All right, you shall have the prescription."

Burns wrote rapidly, resting the small leather-bound book on his knee, his foot on an iron rail of the fence which kept passengers from crowding. He read over what he had written, his face sober, his eyes intent. He scrawled a nearly indecipherable "*Burns*" at the bottom, folded the slip and handed it to his friend. "Put it away till you're ready to get it filled," he advised.

The two shook hands, gripping tightly and looking straight into each other's eyes.

"Thank you, Red, for it all," said Gardner Coolidge. "There have been minutes when I felt differently, but I understand you better now. And I see why your waiting room is full of patients even on a stormy day."

"No, you don't," denied Red Pepper

Burns stoutly. "If you saw me take their heads off you'd wonder that they ever came again. Plenty of them don't—and I don't blame them—when I've cooled off."

Coolidge smiled. "You never lie awake thinking over what you've said or done, do you, Red? Bygones are bygones with a man like you. You couldn't do your work if they weren't!"

A peculiar look leaped into Burns's eyes. "That's what the outsiders always think," he answered briefly.

"Isn't it true?"

"You may as well go on thinking it is—and so may the rest. What's the use of explaining oneself, or trying to? Better to go on looking unsympathetic—and suffering, sometimes, more than all one's patients put together!"

Coolidge stared at the other man. His face showed suddenly certain grim lines which Coolidge had not noticed there before—lines written by endurance, nothing less. But even as the patient looked the physician's expression changed again. His sternly set lips relaxed into a smile, he pointed to a motioning porter.

"Time to be off, Cooly," he said. "Mind you let me know how—you are. Good luck—the best of it!"

In the train Coolidge had no sooner settled himself than he read Burns's prescription. He had a feeling that it would be different from other prescriptions, and so it proved:

Rx

Walk five miles every evening.

Drink no sort of stimulant, except one cup of coffee at breakfast.

Begin to make plans for the cottage. Don't let it turn out a palace.

Ask the good Lord every night to keep you from being a proud fool.

Burns.

CHAPTER II

Little Hungary

"Not hungry, Red? After all that cold drive to-day? Would you like to have Cynthia make you something special, dear?"

R.P. Burns, M.D., shook his head. "No, thanks." He straightened in his chair, where he sat at the dinner table opposite his wife. He took up his knife and fork again and ate valiantly a mouthful or two of the tempting food upon his plate, then he laid the implements down decisively. He put his elbow on the table and leaned his head upon his hand. "I'm just too blamed tired to eat, that's all," he said.

"Then don't try. I'm quite through, too. Come in the living room and lie down a little. It's such a stormy night there may be nobody in."

Ellen slipped her hand through his arm and led the way to the big blue couch facing the fireplace. He dropped upon it with a sigh of fatigue. His wife sat down beside him and began to pass her fingers lightly through his heavy hair, with the touch which usually soothed him into slumber if no interruptions came to summon him. But to-night her ministrations seemed to have little effect, for he lay staring at a certain picture on the wall with eyes which evidently saw beyond it into some trying memory.

"Is the whole world lying heavy on your shoulders to-night, Red?" Ellen asked presently, knowing that sometimes speech proved a relief from thought.

He nodded. "The whole world—millions of tons of it. It's just because I'm tired. There's no real reason why I should take this day's work harder than usual—except that I lost the Anderson case this morning. Poor start for the day, eh?"

"But you knew you must lose it. Nobody could have saved that poor creature."

"I suppose not. But I wanted to save him just the same. You see, he particularly wanted to live, and he had pinned his whole faith to me. He wouldn't give it up that I could do the miracle. It hurts to disappoint a faith like that."

"Of course it does," she said gently. "But you must try to forget now, Red, because of to-morrow. There will be people to-morrow who need you as much as he did."

"That's just what I'd like to forget," he murmured. "Everything's gone wrong to-day—it'll go worse to-morrow."

She knew it was small use to try to combat this mood, so unlike his usual optimism, but frequent enough of occurrence to make her understand that there is no depression like that of the habitually buoyant, once it takes firm hold. She left him presently and went to sit by the reading lamp, looking through current magazines in hope of finding some article sufficiently attractive to capture his interest, and divert his heavy thoughts. His eyes rested absently on her as she sat there, a charming, comradely figure in her simple home dinner attire, with the light on her dark hair and the exquisite curve of her cheek.

It was a fireside scene of alluring comfort, the two central figures of such opposite characteristics, yet so congenial. The night outside was very cold, the wind blowing stormily in great gusts which now and then howled down the chimney, making the warmth and cheer within all the more appealing.

Suddenly Ellen, hunting vainly for the page she sought, lifted her head, to see her husband lift his at the same instant.

"Music?" she questioned. "Where can it come from? Not outside on such a night as this?"

"Did you hear it, too? I've been thinking it my imagination."

"It must be the wind, but—no, it *is* music!"

She rose and went to the window, pushing aside draperies and setting her face to the frosty pane. The next instant she called in a startled way:

"Oh, Red—come here!"

He came slowly, but the moment he caught sight of the figure in the storm outside his langour vanished.

"Good heavens! The poor beggar! We must have him in."

He ran to the hall and the outer door, and Ellen heard his shout above the howling of the wind.

"Come in—come in!"

She reached the door into the hall as the slender young figure stumbled up the steps, a violin clutched tight in fingers purple with cold. She saw the stiff lips break into a frozen smile as her husband laid his hand upon the thinly clad shoulder and drew the youth where he could close the door.

"Why didn't you come to the door and ring, instead of fiddling out there in the cold!" demanded Burns. "Do you think we're heathen, to shut anybody out on a night like this?"

The boy shook his head. He was a boy in size, though the maturity of his thin face suggested that he was at least nineteen or twenty years old. His dark eyes gleamed out of hollow sockets, and his black hair, curling thickly, was rough with neglect. But he had snatched off his ragged soft hat even before he was inside the door, and for all the stiffness of his chilled limbs his attitude, as he stood before his hosts, had the unconscious grace of the foreigner.

"Where do you come from?" Burns asked.

Again the stranger shook his head.

"He can't speak English," said Ellen.

"Probably not—though he may be bluffing. We must warm and feed him, anyhow. Will you have him in here, or shall I take him in the office?"

Ellen glanced again at the shivering youth, noted that the purple hands were clean, even to the nails, and led the way unhesitatingly into the living room with all its beckoning warmth and beauty.

"Good little sport—I knew you would," murmured Burns, as he beckoned the boy after him.

Ellen left the two alone together by the fire, while she went to prepare a tray with Cynthia in the kitchen, filling it with the hearty food Burns himself had left untouched. Big slices of juicy roast beef, two hurriedly warmed sweet potatoes which had been browned in syrup in the Southern style, crisp buttered rolls, and a pot of steaming coffee were on the large tray which Cynthia insisted on carrying to the living-room door for her mistress. Burns, jumping up at sight of her, took the tray, while Ellen cleared a small table, drew up a chair, and summoned the young stranger.

The low bow he made her before he took the chair proclaimed his breeding, as well as the smile of joy which showed the flash of his even white teeth in the firelight. He made a little gesture of gratitude toward both Burns and Ellen, pressing his hands over his heart and then extending them, the expression on his face touching in its starved restraint. Then he fell upon the food, and even though he was plainly ravenous he ate as manneredly as any gentleman. Only by the way he finished each tiniest crumb could they know his extremity.

"By Jove, that beats eating it myself, if I were hungry as a faster on the third day!" Burns exclaimed, as he sat turned away from the beneficiary, his eyes apparently upon the fire. Ellen, from behind the boy, smiled at her husband, noting how completely his air of fatigue had fallen from him. Often before she had observed how any call upon R.P. Burns's sympathies rode down his own need of commiseration.

"Hungarian, I think, don't you?" Burns remarked, as the meal was finished, and the youth rose to bow his thanks once more. This time there was a response. He nodded violently, smiling and throwing out his hands.

"*Ungahree*!" he said, and smiled and nodded again, and said again, "*Ungahree*!"

"He knows that word all right," said Burns, smiling back. "It's a land of musicians. The fiddle's a good one, I'll wager."

He glanced at it as he spoke, and the boy leaped for it, pressing it to his breast. He began to tune it.

"He thinks we want to be paid for his supper," Ellen exclaimed. "Can't you make him understand we should like him to rest first?"

"I'd only convey to him the idea that we didn't want to hear him play, which would be a pity, for we do. If he's the musician he looks, by those eyes and that mouth, we'll be more than paid. Go ahead, Hungary—it'll make you happier than anything we could do for you."

Clearly it would. Burns carried out the tray, and when he returned his guest was standing upon the hearth rug facing Ellen, his bow uplifted. He waited till Burns had thrown himself down on the couch again in a sitting posture, both arms stretched along the back. Then he made his graceful obeisance again, and drew the bow very slowly and softly over the first string. And, at the very first note, the two who were watching him knew what was to come. It was in every line of him, that promise.

It might have been his gratitude that he was voicing, so touching were the strains that followed that first note. The air was unfamiliar, but it sounded like a folk song of his own country, and he put into it all the poignant, peculiar melody of such a song. His tones were exquisite, with the sure touch of the trained violinist inspired and supported by the emotional understanding of the genuine musician.

When he had finished he stood looking downward for a moment, then as Burns said "Bravo!" he smiled as if he understood the word, and lifted his instrument again to his shoulder. This time his bow descended upon the strings with a full note of triumph, and he burst into the brilliant performance of a great masterpiece, playing with a spirit and dash which seemed to transform him. Often his lips parted to show his white teeth, often he swung his whole body into the rhythm of his music, until he seemed a very part of the splendid harmonies he made. His thin cheeks flushed, his hollow eyes grew bright, he smiled, he frowned, he shook his slender shoulders, he even took a stride to right or left as he played on, as if the passion of his performance would not let him rest.

His listeners watched him with sympathetic and comprehending interest. Warmed and fed, his Latin nature leaping up from its deep depression to the exaltation of the hour, the appeal he made to them was intensely pathetic. Burns, even more ardently than his wife, responded to the appeal. He no longer lounged among the pillows of the broad couch; he sat erect, his eyes intent, his lips relaxed, his cares forgot. He was a lover of music, as are many men of his profession, and he was more than ordinarily susceptible to its influences. He drank in the tones of the master, voiced by this devoted interpreter, like wine, and like wine they brought the colour to his face also, and the light to his eyes.

"Jove!" he murmured, as the last note died away, "he's a wonder. He must be older than he looks. How he loves it! He's forgotten that he doesn't know where he's to sleep to-night—but, by all that's fair, *we* know, eh?"

Ellen smiled, with a look of assent. Her own heart was warmly touched. There was a small bedroom upstairs, plainly but comfortably furnished, which was often used for impecunious patients who needed to remain under observation for a day or two. It was at the service of any chance guest, and the chance guest was surely with them to-night. There was no place in the village to which such a vagrant as this might be sent, except the jail, and the jail, for a musician of such quality, was unthinkable. And in the night and storm one would not turn a dog outdoors to hunt for shelter—at least not Red Pepper Burns nor Ellen Burns, his wife.

As if he could not stop, now that he had found ears to listen, the young Hungarian played on. More and more profoundly did his music move him, until it seemed as if he had become the very spirit of the instrument which sung and vibrated under his thin fingers.

"My word, Len, this is too good to keep all to ourselves. Let's have the Macauleys and Chesters over. Then we'll have an excuse for paying the chap a good sum for his work—and somehow I feel that we need an excuse for such a gentleman as he is."

"That's just the thing. I'll ask them."

She was on her way to the telephone when her husband suddenly called after her, "Wait a minute, Len." She turned back, to see the musician, his bow faltering, suddenly lower his violin and lean against his patron, who had leaped to his support. A minute later Burns had him stretched upon the blue couch, and had laid his fingers on the bony wrist.

"Hang me for a simpleton, to feed him like that he's probably not tasted solid food for days. The reaction is too much, of course. He's been playing on his nerve for the last ten minutes, and I, like an idiot, thought it was his emotional temperament."

He ran out of the room and returned with a wine glass filled with liquid, which he administered, his arm under the ragged shoulders. Then he patted the wasted cheek, gone suddenly white except where the excited colour still showed in faint patches.

"You'll be all right, son," he said, smiling down into the frightened eyes, and his tone if not his words seemed to carry reassurance, for the eyes closed with a weary flutter and the gripping fingers relaxed.

"He's completely done," Burns said pityingly. He took one hand in his own and held it in his warm grasp, at which the white lids unclosed again, and the sensitive lips tried to smile.

"I'd no business to let him play so long—I might have known. Poor boy, he's starved for other things than food. Do you suppose anybody's held his hand like this since he left the old country? He thought he'd find wealth and fame in the new one—and this is what he found!"

Ellen stood looking at the pair—her brawny husband, himself "completely done" an hour before, now sitting on the edge of the couch with his new patient's hand in his, his face wearing an expression of keen interest, not a sign of fatigue in his manner; the exhausted young foreigner in his ragged clothing lying on the luxurious couch, his pale face standing out like a fine cameo against the blue velvet of the pillow under his dark head. If a thought of possible contamination for her home's belongings entered her mind it found no lodgment there, so pitiful was her heart.

"Is the room ready upstairs?" Burns asked presently, when he had again noted the feeble action of the pulse under his fingers. "What he needs is rest and sleep, and plenty of both. Like the most of us he's kept up while he had to, and now he's gone to pieces absolutely. To-morrow we can send him to the hospital, perhaps, but for to-night—"

"The room is ready. I sent Cynthia up at once."

"Bless you, you never fail me, do you? Well—we may as well be on our way. He's nearly asleep now."

Burns stood up, throwing off his coat. But Ellen remonstrated.

"Dear, you are so tired to-night. Let me call Jim over to help you carry him up."

A derisive laugh answered her. "Great Cæsar, Len! The chap's a mere bag of bones—and if he were twice as heavy he'd be no weight for me. Jim Macauley would howl at the idea, and no wonder.

Go ahead and open the doors, please, and I'll have him up in a jiffy."

He stooped over the couch, swung the slender figure up into his powerful arms, speaking reassuringly to the eyes which slowly opened in half-stupefied alarm. "It's all right, little Hungary. We're going to put you to bed, like the small lost boy you are. Bring his fiddle, Len—he won't want that out of his sight."

He strode away with his burden, and marched up the stairs as if he were carrying his own two-year-old son. Arrived in the small, comfortable little room at the back of the house he laid his charge on the bed, and stood looking down at him.

"Len, I'll have to go the whole figure," he said—and said it not as if the task he was about to impose upon himself were one that irked him. "Get me hot water and soap and towels, will you? And an old pair of pajamas. I can't put him to bed in his rags."

"Shall I send for Amy?" questioned his wife, quite as if she understood the uselessness of remonstrance.

"Not much. Amy's making out bills for me to-night, we'll not interrupt the good work. Put some bath-ammonia in the water, please—and have it hot."

Half an hour later he called her in to see the work of his hands. She had brought him one of his surgical aprons with the bath equipment. With his sleeves rolled up, his apron well splashed, his coppery hair more or less in disarray from the occasional thrustings of a soapy hand, and his face flushed and eager like a healthy boy's, Red Pepper Burns stood grinning down at his patient. Little Hungary lay in the clean white bed, his pale face shining with soap and happiness, his arms upon the coverlet encased in the blue and white sleeves of Burns's pajamas, the sleeves neatly turned back to accommodate the shortness of his arms. The workman turned to Ellen as she came in.

"Comfy, eh?" he observed briefly.

"Absolutely, I should say, poor dear."

"Ah, you wouldn't have called him that

before the bath. But he is rather a dear now, isn't he? And I think he's younger than I did downstairs. Not over eighteen, at the most, but fully forty in the experiences and hardships that have brought him here. Well, we'll go away and let him rest. Wish I knew the Hungarian for 'good-night,' don't you? Anyway, if he knows any prayers he'll say 'em, I'll venture."

The dark eyes were watching him intently as he spoke, as if their owner longed to know what this kind angel in the form of a big American stranger was saying to him. And when, in leaving him, Burns once more laid an exploring touch upon his wrist, the two thin hands suddenly clutched the strong one and bore it weakly to lips which kissed it fervently.

"Well, that's rather an eloquent thank-you, eh?" murmured Burns, as he patted the hands in reply. "No doubt but he's grateful. Put the fiddle where he can see it in the morning, will you, honey? Open the window pretty well: I've covered him thoroughly, and he has a touch of fever to keep him warm.

Good-night, little Hungary. Luck's with you to-night, to get into this lady's house."

Downstairs by the fireside once more, the signs of his late occupation removed, Burns stretched out an arm for his wife.

"Come sit beside me in the Retreat," he invited, using the name he had long ago given to the luxurious blue couch where he was accustomed, since his marriage, to rest and often to catch a needed nap. He drew the winsome figure close within his arm, resting his red head against the dark one below it. "I don't seem to feel particularly tired, now," he observed. "Curious, isn't it? Fatigue, as I've often noticed, is more mental than physical—with most of us. Your ditch-digger is tired in his back and arms, but the ordinary person is merely tired because his mind tells him he is."

"You are never too tired to rouse yourself for one patient more," was Ellen's answer to this. "The last one seems to cure you of the one before."

Burns's hearty laugh shook them both. "You can't make me out such an enthusiast in my profession as that. I turned away two country calls to-night—too lazy to make 'em."

"But you would have gone if they couldn't have found anybody else."

"That goes without saying—no merit in that. The ethics of the profession have to be lived up to, curse 'em as we may, at times. Len, how are we to get to know something about little Hungary upstairs? Those eyes of his are going to follow me into my dreams to-night."

"I suppose there are Hungarians in town?"

"Not a one that I ever heard of. Plenty in the city, though. The waiter at the Arcadia, where I get lunch when I'm at the hospital, is a Magyar. By Jove, there's an idea! I'll bring Louis out, if Hungary can't get into the hospital to-morrow—and I warn you he probably can't. I shouldn't want him to take a twelve-mile ambulance ride in this weather. That touch of fever may mean simple exhaustion, and it may mean look out for pneumonia, after all the exposure he's had. I'd give something to know how it came into his crazy head to stand and fiddle outside a private house in a January storm. Why didn't he try a cigar shop or some other warm spot where he could pass the hat? That's what Louis must find out for me, eh? Len, that was great music of his, wasn't it? The fellow ought to have a job in a hotel orchestra. Louis and I between us might get him one."

Burns went to bed still working on this problem, and Ellen rejoiced that it had superseded the anxieties of the past day. Next morning he was early at the little foreigner's bedside, to find him resting quietly, the fever gone, and only the intense fatigue remaining, the cure for which was simply rest and food.

"Shall we let him stay till he's fit?" Burns asked his wife.

"Of course. Both Cynthia and Amy are much interested, and between them he will have all he needs."

"And I'll bring Louis out, if I have to pay for a waiter to take his place," promised Burns.

He was as good as his word. When he returned that afternoon from the daily visit to the city hospital, where he had always many patients, he brought with him in the powerful roadster which he drove himself a dark-faced, pointed moustached countryman of little Hungary, who spoke tolerable English, and was much pleased and flattered to be of service to the big doctor whom he was accustomed to serve in his best manner.

Taken to the bedside, Louis gazed down at its occupant with condescending but comprehending eyes, and spoke a few words which caused the thin face on the pillow to break into smiles of delight, as the eager lips answered in the same tongue. Question and answer followed in quick succession and Louis was soon able to put Burns in possession of a few significant facts.

"He say he come to dis countree October. Try find work New York—no good. He start to valk to countree, find vork farm. Bad time. Seeck, cold, hungree. Fear he spoil hands for veolinn—dat's vhy he not take vork on road, vat he could get. He museecian—good one."

"Does he say that?" Burns asked, amused.

Louis nodded. "Many museecians in Hungary. Franz come from Budapest. No poor museecians dere. Budapest great ceety—better Vienna, Berlin, Leipsic—oh, yes! See, I ask heem."

He spoke to the boy again, evidently putting a meaning question, for again the other responded with ardour, using his hands to emphasize his assertion—for assertion it plainly was.

Louis laughed. "He say ze countree of Franz Liszt know no poor museeck. He named for Franz Liszt. He play beeg museeck for you and ze ladee last night. So?"

"He did—and took us off our feet. Tell him, will you?"

"He no un'erstand," laughed Louis, "eef I tell him 'off de feet.'"

"That's so—no American idioms yet for him, eh? Well, say he made us very happy with his wonderful music. I'll wager that will get over to him."

Plainly it did, to judge by the eloquence

of Franz's eyes and his joyous smile. With quick speech he responded.

"He say," reported Louis, "he vant to vork for you. No wagees till he plees you. He do anyting. You van' heem?"

"Well, I'll have to think about that," Burns temporized. "But tell him not to worry. We'll find a job before we let him go. He ought to play in a restaurant or theatre, oughtn't he, Louis?"

Louis shook his head. "More men nor places," he said. "But ve see—ve see."

"All right. Now ask him how he came to stand in front of my house in the storm and fiddle."

To this Louis obtained a long reply, at which he first shook his head, then nodded and laughed, with a rejoinder which brought a sudden rush of tears to the black eyes below. Louis turned to Burns.

"He say man lead heem here, make heem stand by window, make sign to heem to play. I tell heem man knew soft heart eenside."

To the edge of his coppery hair the blood rushed into the face of Red Pepper Burns. Whether he would be angry or amused was for the moment an even chance, as Ellen, watching him, understood. Then he shook his fist with a laugh.

"Just wait till I catch that fellow!" he threatened. "A nice way out of his own obligations to a starving fellow man."

He sent Louis back to town on the electric car line, with a round fee in his pocket, and the instruction to leave no stone unturned to find Franz work for his violin, himself promising to aid him in any plan he might formulate.

In three days the young Hungarian was so far himself that Burns had him downstairs to sit by the office fire, and a day more put him quite on his feet. Careful search had discovered a temporary place for him in a small hotel orchestra, whose second violin was ill, and Burns agreed to take him into the city. The evening before he was to go, Ellen invited a number of her friends and neighbours in to hear Franz play.

Dressed in a well-fitting suit of blue serge Franz looked a new being. The suit had been contributed by Arthur Chester, Burns's neighbour and good friend next door upon the right, and various other accessories had been supplied by James Macauley, also Burns's neighbour and good friend next door upon the left and the husband of Martha Macauley, Ellen's sister. Even so soon the rest and good food had filled out the deepest hollows in the emaciated cheeks, and happiness had lighted the sombre eyes. Those eyes followed Burns about with the adoring gaze of a faithful dog.

"It's evident you've attached one more devoted follower to your train, Red," whispered Winifred Chester, in an interval of the violin playing.

"Well, he's a devotee worth having," answered Burns, watching his protégé as Franz looked over a pile of music with Ellen, signifying his pleasure every time they came upon familiar sheets. The two had found common ground in their love of the most emotional of all the arts, and Ellen had discovered rare delight in accompanying that ardent violin in some of the scores both knew and loved.

"He's as handsome as a picture to-night, isn't he?" Winifred pursued. "How Arthur's old blue suit transforms him. And wasn't it clever of Ellen to have him wear that soft white shirt with the rolling collar and flowing black tie? It gives him the real musician's look."

"Trust you women to work for dramatic effects," murmured Burns. "Here we go—and I'll wager it'll be something particularly telling, judging by the way they both look keyed up to it. Ellen plays like a virtuoso herself to-night, doesn't she?"

"It's enough to inspire any one to have that fiddle at her shoulder," remarked James Macauley, who, hanging over the couch, had been listening to this bit of talk.

The performance which followed captured them all, even practical and energetic Martha Macauley, who had often avowed that she considered the study of music a waste of time in a busy world.

"Though I think, after all," she observed

to Arthur Chester, who lounged by her side, revelling in the entertainment with the zest of the man who would give his whole time to affairs like these if it were not necessary for him to make a living at the practice of some more prosaic profession, "it's quite as much the interest of having such a stagey character performing for us as it is his music. Did you ever see any human being throw his whole soul into anything like that? One couldn't help but watch him if he weren't making a sound."

"It's certainly refreshing, in a world where we all try to cover up our real feelings, to see anybody give himself away so naïvely as that," Chester replied. "But there's no doubt about the quality of his music. He was born, not made. And, by George, Len certainly plays up to him. I didn't know she had it in her, for all I've been admiring her accomplishments for four years."

"Ellen's all temperament, anyway," said Ellen's sister.

Chester looked at her curiously. Martha was a fine-looking young woman, in a very wholesome and clean-cut fashion. There was no feminine artfulness in the way she bound her hair smoothly upon her head, none in the plain cut of her simple evening attire, absolutely none in her manner. Glancing from Martha to her sister, as he had often done before in wonderment at the contrast between them, he noted as usual how exquisitely Ellen was dressed, though quite as simply, in a way, as her practical sister. But in every line of her smoke-blue silken frock was the most subtle art, as Chester, who had a keen eye for such matters and a fastidious taste, could readily recognize. From the crown of her dark head to the toe of the blue slipper with which she pressed the pedal of the great piano which she had brought from her old home in the South, she was a picture to feast one's eyes upon.

"Give me temperament, then—and let some other fellow take the common sense," mused Arthur Chester to himself. "Ellen has both, and Red's in luck. It was a great day for him when the lovely young widow came his way—and he knows it. What a home she makes him—what a home!"

His eyes roved about the beautiful living room, as they had often done before. His own home, next door, was comfortable and more than ordinarily attractive, but he knew of no spot in the town which possessed the subtle charm of this in which he sat. His wife, Winifred, was always trying to reproduce within their walls the indefinable quality which belonged to everything Ellen touched, and always saying in despair, "It's no use—Ellen is Ellen, and other people can't be like her."

"Better let it go at that," her husband sometimes responded. "You're good enough for me." Which was quite true, for Winifred Chester was a peculiarly lovable young woman. He noted afresh to-night that beside Martha Macauley's somewhat heavy good looks Winifred seemed a creature of infinite and delightful variety.

Perhaps the music had made them all more or less analytic, for in an interval James Macauley, comfortably ensconced in a great winged chair for which he was accustomed to steer upon entering this room, where he was nearly as much at home as within his own walls, remarked, "What is there about music like that that sets you to thinking everybody in sight is about the best ever?"

"Does it have that effect on you?" queried Burns, lazily, from the blue couch. "That's a good thing for a fellow of a naturally critical disposition."

"Critical, am I? Why, within a week I paid you the greatest compliment in my power."

"Really!"

"If it hadn't been for me this company would never have been gathered, to listen to these wondrous strains."

"How's that?" Burns turned on him a suddenly interested eye.

"Oh, I'm not telling. It's enough that the thing came about." Macauley looked around for general approbation.

Red Pepper sat up. "It was you stood the poor beggar up under my window, on that howling night, was it, Jim? I've been looking for the man that did it."

"Why," said Macauley comfortably, "the chap asked me to point him to a doctor's office—said he had a bit of a cold. I said you were the one and only great and original M.D. upon earth, and as luck would have it he was almost at your door. I said that if he didn't find you in he should come over to my house and we would fix him up with cough drops. He thanked me and passed on. As luck would have it you were in."

Red Pepper glared at him. A chuckle from Arthur Chester caused him to turn his eyes that way. He scrutinized his guests in turn, and detected signs of mirth. Winifred Chester's pretty shoulders were shaking. Martha Macauley's lips were pressed close together. The others were all smiling.

Burns turned upon Winifred, who sat nearest. "Tell me the truth about this thing," he commanded.

She shook her head, but she got no peace until at length she gave him the tale.

"Arthur and I were over at Jim's. He came in and said a wager was up among some men outside as to whether if that poor boy came and fiddled under your window you'd take him in and keep him over night. Somebody'd been saying things against you, down street somewhere—" she hesitated, glancing at her husband, who nodded, and said, "Go on—he'll have it out of us now, anyhow."

"They said," she continued, "that you were the most brutal surgeon in the State, and that you hadn't any heart. Some of them made this wager, and they all sneaked up here behind the one that steered Franz to your window."

Burns's quick colour had leaped to his face at this recital, as they were all accustomed to see it, but for an instant he made no reply. Winifred looked at him steadily, as one who was not afraid.

"We were all in a dark window watching. If you hadn't taken him in we would. But—O Red! We knew—we knew that heart of yours."

"And who started that wager business?" Burns inquired, in a muffled voice.

"Why, Jim, of course. Who else would take such a chance?"

"Was it a serious wager?"

"Of course it was."

"Even odds?"

"No, it was Jim against the crowd. And for a ridiculously high stake."

Red Pepper glared at James Macauley once more. "You old pirate!" he growled. "How dared you take such a chance on me? And when you know I'm death on that gambling propensity of yours?"

"I know you are," replied Macauley, with a satisfied grin. "And you know perfectly well I haven't staked a red copper for a year. But that sort of talk I overheard was too much for me. Besides, I ran no possible risk for my money. I was betting on a sure thing."

Burns got up, amidst the affectionate laughter which followed this explanation, and walked over to where Franz stood, his eager eyes fixed upon his new and adored friend, who, he somehow divined, was the target for some sort of badinage.

"Little Hungary," he said, smiling into the uplifted, boyish face, with his hand on the slender shoulder, "it came out all right that time, but don't you ever play under my window again in a January blizzard. If you do, I'll kick you out into the storm!"

CHAPTER III

Anne Linton's Temperature

"Is Doctor Burns in?"

"He's not in. He will be here from two till five this afternoon. Could you come then?" Miss Mathewson regarded the young stranger at the door with more than ordinary interest. The face which was lifted to her was one of quite unusual beauty, with astonishing eyes under resolute dark brows, though the hair which showed from under the small and close-fitting hat of black was of a wonderful and contradictory colour. It was almost the shade, it occurred to Amy Mathewson, of that which thatched the head of Red Pepper Burns himself, but it was more picturesque hair than his, finer of texture, with a hint of curl. The mass of it which showed at the back as the stranger turned her head away for a moment, evidently hesitating over her next course of action, had in it tints of bronze which were more beautiful than Burns's coppery hues.

"Would you care to wait?" inquired Miss

Mathewson, entirely against her own principles.

It was not quite one o'clock, and Burns always lunched in the city, after his morning at the hospital, and reached home barely in time for those afternoon village office hours which began at two. His assistant did not as a rule encourage the arrival of patients in the office as early as this, knowing that they were apt to become impatient and aggrieved by their long wait. But something about the slightly drooping figure of the girl before her, in her black clothes, with a small handbag on her arm, and a look of appeal on her face, suggested to the experienced nurse that here was a patient who must not be turned away.

The girl looked up eagerly. "If I might," she said in a tone of relief. "I really have nowhere to go until I have seen the Doctor."

Miss Mathewson led her in and gave her the most comfortable chair in the room, a big, half shabby leather armchair, near the fireplace and close beside a broad table whereon the latest current magazines were arranged in orderly piles. The girl sank into the chair as if its wide arms were welcome after a weary morning. She looked up at Miss Mathewson with a faint little smile.

"I haven't been sitting much to-day," she said.

"This first spring weather makes every one feel rather tired," replied Amy, noting how heavy were the shadows under the brown eyes with their almost black lashes—an unusual combination with the undeniably russet hair.

From her seat at the desk, where she was posting Burns's day book, the nurse observed without seeming to do so that the slim figure in the old armchair sat absolutely without moving, except once when the head resting against the worn leather turned so that the cheek lay next it. And after a very short time Miss Mathewson realized that the waiting patient had fallen asleep. She studied her then, for something about the young stranger had aroused her interest.

The girl was obviously poor, for the black suit, though carefully pressed, was of cheap material, the velvet on the small black hat had been caught in more than one shower, and the black gloves had been many times painstakingly mended. The small feet alone showed that their owner had allowed herself one luxury, that of good shoes—and the daintiness of those feet made a strong appeal to the observer.

As for the face resting against the chair back, it was flushed after a fashion which suggested illness rather than health, and Miss Mathewson realized presently that the respiration of the sleeper was not quite what it should be. Whether this were due to fatigue or coming illness she could not tell.

Half-past one! The first early caller was slowing a small motor at the curb outside when Amy Mathewson gently touched the girl's arm. "Come into the other room, please," she said.

The brown eyes opened languidly. The black-gloved hand clutched at the handbag, and the girl rose. "I'm so sorry," she murmured. "I don't know how I came to go to sleep."

"You were tired out. If I had known I should have brought you in here before," Amy said, leading her into the consulting room. "It is still half an hour before Doctor Burns will be in, and you must lie here on his couch while you wait."

"Oh, thank you, but I ought not to go to sleep. I—have you just a minute to spare? I should like to show you a little book I am selling—"

Miss Mathewson suffered a sudden revulsion of feeling. So this girl was only a book agent. First on the list of what by two o'clock would be a good-sized assemblage of waiting patients, she must not be allowed to take Doctor Burns's time to exploit her wares. Yet, even as Amy regretted having brought a book agent into this inner sanctum, the girl looked up from searching in her handbag and seemed to recognize the prejudice she had excited.

"Oh, but I'm a patient, too," she said with a little smile. "I didn't expect to take the Doctor's time telling him about the book. But you—I thought you might be interested. It's a little book of bedtime stories for children. They are very jolly little tales. Would you care to see it?"

Now Amy Mathewson was the fortunate or unfortunate—as you happen to regard such things—possessor of a particularly warm heart, and the result of this appeal was that she took the book away with her into the outer office, promising to look it over if the seller of it would lie down upon the couch and rest quietly. She was convinced that the girl was much more than weary—she was very far from well. The revealing light of that consulting room had struck upon the upturned face and had shown Miss Mathewson's trained eyes certain signs which alarmed her.

So it came about that Red Pepper Burns, coming in ruddy from his twelve-mile dash home, and feeling particularly fit for the labours of the afternoon in consequence of having found every hospital patient of his own on the road to recovery—two of them having taken a right-about-face from a condition which the day before had pointed toward trouble—discovered his first office patient lying fast asleep upon the consulting room couch.

"She seemed so worn out I put her here," explained Miss Mathewson, standing beside him. "She falls asleep the moment she is off her feet."

"Hm—m," was his reply as he thrust his arms into his white office-jacket. "Well, best wake her up, though it seems a pity. Looks as if she'd been on a hunger strike, eh?" he added under his breath.

Miss Mathewson had the girl awake again in a minute, and she sat up, an expression of contrition crossing her face as she caught sight of the big doctor at the other side of the room, his back toward her. When Burns turned, at Amy's summons, he beheld the slim figure sitting straight on the edge of the broad couch, the brown eyes fixed on him.

"Tired out?" he asked pleasantly. "Take this chair, please, so I can see all you have to tell me—and a few things you don't tell me."

It did not take him long. His eyes on the face which was too flushed, his fingers on the pulse which beat too fast, his thermometer registering a temperature too high, all told him that here was work for him. The questions he asked brought replies which confirmed his fears. Nothing in his manner indicated, however, that he was doing considerable quick thinking. His examination over, he sat back in his chair and began a second series of questions, speaking in a more than ordinarily quiet but cheerful way.

"Will you tell me just a bit about your personal affairs?" he asked. "I understand that you come from some distance. Have you a home and family?"

"No family—for the last two years, since my father died."

"And no home?"

"If I am ill, Doctor Burns, I will look after myself."

He studied her. The brown eyes met the scrutinizing hazel ones without flinching. Whether or not the spirit flinched he could not be sure. The hazel eyes were very kindly.

"You have relatives somewhere whom we might let know of this?"

She shook her head determinedly. Her head lifted ever so little.

"You are quite alone in the world?"

"For all present purposes—yes, Doctor Burns."

"I can't just believe," he said gently, "that it is not very important to somebody to know if you are ill."

"It is just my affair," she answered with equal courtesy of manner but no less finally. "Believe me, please—and tell me what to do. Shall I not be better to-morrow—or in a day or two?"

He was silent for a moment. Then, "It is not a time for you to be without friends," said Red Pepper Burns. "I will prove to you that you have them at hand. After that you will find there are others. I am going to take you to a pleasant place I know of, where you will have nothing to do but to lie still and rest and get well. The best of nurses will look after you. You will obey orders for a little—my orders, if you want to trust me—"

"Where is this place?" The question was a little breathless.

"Where do you guess?"

"In—a hospital?"

"In one of the best in the world."

"I am—pretty ill then?"

"It's a bit of a wonder," said Burns in his quietest tone, "how you have kept around these last four days. I wish you hadn't."

"If I hadn't," said the girl rather faintly, "I shouldn't have been in this town and I shouldn't have come to Doctor Burns. So—I'm glad I did."

"Good!" said Burns, smiling. "It's fine to start with the confidence of one's patient. I'm glad you're going to trust me. Now we'll take you to another room where you can lie down again till my office hours are over and I can run into the city with you."

He rose, beckoning. But his patient protested: "Please tell me how to get there. I can go perfectly well. My head is better, I think."

"That's lucky. But the first of my orders Miss Linton, is that you come with me now."

He summoned Miss Mathewson, gave her directions, and dismissed the two. In ten minutes the heavy eyes were again closed, while their owner lay motionless again upon a bed in an inner room which was often used for such purposes.

"I'm sorry I can't take her in now," Burns said to Amy presently in an interval between patients. "I don't want to call the ambulance out here for a walking case, and there's no need of startling her with it, anyhow. I wish I had some way to send her."

"Mr. Jordan King just came into the office. His car is outside. Couldn't he take her in?"

"Of course he could—and would, I've no doubt. He's only after his mother's prescription. Send him in here next, will you, please?"

To the tall, well-built, black-eyed young man who answered this summons in some surprise at being admitted before his turn, Burns spoke crisply:

"Here's the prescription, Jord, and you'll have to take it to Wood's to get it filled. I hope it'll do your mother a lot of good, but I'm not promising till I've tried it out pretty well. Now will you do me a favour?"

"Anything you like, Doctor."

"Thanks. I'm sending a patient to the hospital—a stranger stranded here ill. She ought not to be out of bed another hour, though she walked to the office and would walk away again if I'd let her—which I won't. I can't get off for three hours yet. Will you take her in to the Good Samaritan for me? I'll telephone ahead, and some one will meet her at the door. All right?"

He looked up. Jordan King—young civil engineer of rising reputation in spite of the family wealth which would have made him independent of his own exertions, if he could possibly have been induced by an adoring, widowed mother to remain under her wing—stood watching him with a smile on his character-betraying lips.

"You ought to have an executive position of some sort, Doctor Burns," he observed, "you're so strong on orders. I've got mine. Where's the lady? Do I have to be silent or talkative? Is she to have pillows? Am I to help her out?"

"She'll walk out—but that and the walk in will be the last she'll take for some time. Talk as much as you like; it'll help her to forget that she's alone in the world at present except for us. Go out to your car; I'll send her out with Miss Mathewson."

Burns turned to his desk, and King obediently went out. Five minutes later, as he stood waiting beside his car, a fine but hard-used roadster of impressive lines and plenty of power, the office nurse and her patient emerged. King noted in some surprise the slender young figure, the interest-compelling face with its too vivid colour in cheeks that looked as if ordinarily they were white, the apparel which indicated lack of means, though the bearing of the wearer unmistakably suggested social training.

"I thought she'd be an elderly one somehow," he said in congratulation of himself. "Jolly, what hair! Poor little girl; she does look sick—but plucky. Hope I can get her in all right."

Outwardly he was the picture of respectful attention as Miss Mathewson presented him, calling the girl "Miss Linton," and bidding him wrap her warmly against the spring wind.

"I'll take the best care of her I know," he promised with a friendly smile. He tucked a warm rug around her, taking special pains with her small feet, whose well-chosen covering he did not fail to note. "All right?" he asked as he finished.

"Very comfortable, thank you. It's ever so kind of you."

"Glad to do anything for Doctor Burns," King responded, taking his place beside her. "Now shall we go fast or slow?"

"Just as you like, please. I don't feel very ill just now, and this air is so good on my face."

CHAPTER IV

Two Red Heads

Jordan King set his own speed in the powerful roadster, reflecting that Miss Linton, to judge from her worn black clothes, was probably not accustomed to motoring and so making the pace a moderate one. Fast or slow, it would not take long to cover the twelve miles over the macadamized road to the hospital in the city, and if it was to be her last bath in the good outdoors for some time, as the doctor had said—King drew a long breath, filling his own sturdy lungs with the balmy yet potent April air, feeling very sorry for the unknown little person by his side.

"Would you rather I didn't talk?" he inquired when a mile or two had been covered in silence.

She lifted her eyes to his, and for the first time he got a good look into them. They were very wonderful eyes, and none the less wonderful because of the fever which made them almost uncannily brilliant between their dark lashes.

"Oh, I wish you would talk, if you don't mind!" she answered—and he noted as he had at first how warmly pleasant were the tones of her voice, which was a bit deeper than one would have expected. "I've heard nobody talk for days—except to say they didn't care to buy my book."

"Your book? Have you written a book?"

"I'm selling one." This astonished him, but he did not let it show. It was certainly enough to make any girl ill to have to go about selling books. He wondered how it happened. She opened her handbag and took out the small book. "I don't want to sell you one," she said. "You wouldn't have any use for it. It's a little set of stories for children."

"But I do want to buy one," he protested. "I've a lot of nieces and nephews always coming at me for stories."

She shook her head. "You can't buy one. I'd like to give you one if you would take it, to show you how I appreciate this beautiful drive."

"Of course I'll take it," he said quickly, "and delighted at the chance." He slipped the book into his pocket. "As for the drive, it's much jollier not to be covering the ground alone. I wish, though—" and he stopped, feeling that he was probably going to say the wrong thing.

She seemed to know what it would have been. "You're sorry to be taking me to the hospital?" she suggested. "You needn't be. I didn't want to go, just at first, but then—I felt I could trust the Doctor. He was so kind, and his hair was so like mine, he seemed like a sort of big older brother."

"Red Pepper Burns seems like that to a lot of people, including myself. I don't look like much of a candidate for illness, but I've had an accident or two, and he's pulled me through in great shape. You're right in trusting him and you can keep right on, to the last ditch—" He stopped short again, with an inward thrust at himself for being so blundering in his suggestions to this girl, who, for all he knew, might be on her way to that "last ditch" from which not even Burns could save her.

But the girl herself seemed to have paused at his first phrase. "What did you call the Doctor?" she asked, turning her eyes upon him again.

"What did I—oh! 'Red Pepper.' Yes—I've no business to call him that, of course, and I don't to his face, though his friends who are a bit older than I usually do, and people speak of him that way. It's his hair, of course—and—well, he has rather a quick temper. People with that coloured hair—But you're wrong in saying yours is like his," he added quickly.

For the first time he saw a smile touch her lips. "So he has a quick temper," she mused. "I'm glad of that—I have one myself. It goes with the hair surely enough."

"It goes with some other things," ventured Jordan King, determined, if he made any more mistakes, to make them on the side of encouragement. "Pluck, and endurance, and keeping jolly when you don't feel so—if you don't mind my saying it."

"One has to have a few of those things to start out into the world with," said Miss Linton slowly, looking straight ahead again.

"One certainly does. Doctor Burns understands that as well as any man I know. And he likes to find those things in other people." Then with tales of some of the Doctor's experiences which young King had heard he beguiled the way; and by the time he had told Miss Linton a story or two about certain experiences of his own in the Rockies, the car was approaching the city. Presently they were drawing up before the group of wide-porched, long buildings, not unattractive in aspect, which formed the hospital known as the Good Samaritan.

"It's a pretty good place," announced King in a matter-of-fact way, though inwardly he was suffering a decided pang of sympathy for the young stranger he was to leave within its walls. "And the Doctor said he'd have some one meet us who knew all about you, so there'd be no fuss."

He leaped out and came around to her side. She began to thank him once more, but he cut her short. "I'm going in with you, if I may," he said. "Something might go wrong about their understanding, and I could save you a bit of bother."

She made no objection, and he helped her out. He kept his hand under her arm as they went up the steps, and did not let her go until they were in a small reception room, where they were asked to wait for a minute. He realized now more than he had done before her weakness and the sense of loneliness that was upon her. He stood beside her, hat in hand, wishing he had some right to let her know more definitely than he had ventured to do how sorry he was for her, and how she could count on his thinking about her as a brother might while she was within these walls.

But Burns's message evidently had taken effect, as his messages usually did, for after a very brief wait two figures in uniform appeared, one showing the commanding presence of a person in authority, the other wearing the pleasantly efficient aspect of the active nurse. Miss Linton was to be taken to her room at once, the necessary procedure for admittance being attended to later.

Miss Linton seemed to know something about hospitals, for she offered instant remonstrance. "It's a mistake, I think," she said, lifting her head as if it were very heavy, but speaking firmly. "I prefer not to have a room. Please put me in your least expensive ward."

The person in authority smiled. "Doctor Burns said room," she returned. "Nobody here is accustomed to dispute Doctor Burns's orders."

"But I must dispute them," persisted the girl. "I am not—willing—to take a room."

"Don't concern yourself about that now," said the other. "You can settle it with the Doctor when he comes by and by."

Jordan King inwardly chuckled. "I wonder if it's going to be a case of two red heads," he said to himself. "I'll bet on R.P."

The nurse put her arm through Miss Linton's. "Come," she said gently. "You ought not to be standing."

The girl turned to King, and put out her small hand in its mended glove. He grasped it and dared to give it a strong pressure, and to say in a low tone: "It'll be all right, you know. Keep a stiff upper lip. We're not going to forget you." He very nearly said "I."

"Good-bye," she said. "I shall not forget how kind you've been."

Then she was gone through the big door, the tall nurse beside her supporting steps which seemed suddenly to falter, and King was staring after her, feeling his heart contract with sympathy.

Four hours later Anne Linton opened her eyes, after an interval of unconsciousness which had seemed to the nurse who looked in now and then less like a sleep than a stupor, to find a pair of broad shoulders within her immediate horizon, and to feel the same lightly firm pressure on her wrist that she had felt before that afternoon. She looked up slowly into Burns's eyes.

"Not so bad, is it?" said his low and reassuring voice. "Bed more comfortable than doctor's office chairs? Won't mind if you don't ring any door bells to-morrow? Just let everything go and don't worry—and you'll be all right."

"This room—" began the weary young voice—she was really much more weary now that she had stopped trying to keep up than seemed at all reasonable—"I can't possibly—"

"It's just the place for you. Don't do any thinking on that point. You know you agreed to take my orders, and this is one of them."

"But I can't possibly—"

"I said they were my orders," repeated Burns. "But that was a misstatement. They're the orders of some one else, more powerful than I am under this roof—and that's saying something, I assure you. I think you'll have to meet my wife. She's come on purpose to see you. She was away when you were at the office."

He beckoned, and another figure moved quietly into range of the brown eyes which were smoldering with the first advances of the fever. This figure came around to the other side of the narrow high bed and sat down beside it. Miss Linton looked into the face, as it seemed to her, of one of the most attractive women she had ever seen. It was a face which looked down at her with the sweetest sympathy in its expression, and yet with that same high cheer which was in the face of the man on the other side of the bed.

"My dear little girl," said a low, rich voice, "this is my room, and I often have the pleasure of seeing my special friends use it. And I come to see them here. When you are getting well, as you will be by and by, I can have much nicer talks with you than if you were in a ward. Now that you understand, you will let me have my way?".

The burning brown eyes looked into the soft black ones for a full minute, then, with a long-drawn breath, the tense expression in the stranger's relaxed. "I see," said the weary voice. "You are used to having your way—just as he is. I'll have to let you because I haven't any strength left to fight with. You are wonderfully kind. But—I'm not a little girl."

Ellen Burns smiled. "We'll play you are, for a while," she said. "And—I want you to know that, little or big, you are my friend. So now you have both Doctor Burns and me, and you are not alone any more."

The heavy lashes closed over the brown eyes, and the lids were held tightly shut as if to keep tears back. Seeing this, Ellen rose.

"Red," she said, "are you going to let us have Miss Arden?"

"Won't anybody else do?"

"Do you need her badly somewhere else?"

"If there were ten of her I could use them all!" declared her husband emphatically.

"Nevertheless—"

Red Pepper Burns got up. He summoned a nurse waiting just outside the door. "Please send Miss Arden here for a minute," he requested. Then he turned back. "Are you satisfied with your power?" he asked his wife.

She nodded. "Quite. But I think you feel, as I do, that this is one of the ten places where she will be better than another."

"She's a wonder, all right."

The patient in the bed presently was bidden to look at her new nurse, one who was to take care of her much of the time. She lifted her heavy eyes unwillingly, then she drew another deep breath of relief. "I would rather have you," she murmured to the serene brow, the kind eyes, the gently smiling lips of the girl who stood beside her.

"There's a tribute," laughed Burns softly. "They all feel like that when they look at you, Selina. And what Mrs. Burns wants she usually gets. You may special this case to-night, if you are ready to begin night duty again."

"I am quite ready," said Miss Arden.

Burns turned to the bed again. "You are in the best hands we have to give you," he said. "You are to trust everything to those hands. Good-night. I'll see you in the morning."

"Good-night, dear," whispered Mrs. Burns, bending for an instant over the bed.

"Oh you angels!" murmured the girl as they left her, her eyes following them.

It was ten days later, in the middle of a wonderful night in early May, that Miss Arden, beginning to be sure that the case which had interested her so much was going to give her a hard time before it should be through, listened to words which roused in her deeper wonder than she had yet felt for the most unusual patient she had had in a long time. Although there was as yet nothing that could be called real delirium, a tendency to talk in a light-headed sort of way was becoming noticeable. Sitting by the window, the one light in the room deeply shaded, she heard the voice suddenly say:

> "This evens things up a little, doesn't it? I know a little more about it now—you must realize that, if you are keeping track of me—and I know you are—you would—even from another world. Things aren't fair—they aren't. That you should have to suffer all you did, to bring you to that pass—while I—But I know a good deal about it now—really I do. And I'm going to know more. I didn't sell a single book to-day. You had lots of such days, didn't you? Poor—pale—tired—heartsick—heartbroken girl!"

A little mirthless laugh sounded from the bed. "I wonder how many people ever let a person who is selling something at the door get into the house. And if they let her in, do they ever, *ever* ask her to sit down? The places where I've stood, telling them about the book, while they were telling me they didn't want it—stood and stood—and stood—with great easy chairs in sight! Oh, that chair in my doctor's office—it was the first chair I'd sat in that whole morning. I went to sleep in it, I think."

There followed a long silence, as if the thought of sleep had brought it on. But then the rambling talk began again.

> "His hair is red—red, like mine. I think that's why his heart is so warm. Yet her heart is warm, too, and her hair is almost black. The other man's hair was pretty dark, too, and his heart seemed—well, not exactly cold. Did he send me some daffodils the other day? I can't seem to remember. It seems as if I had seen some—pretty things—lovely, springy things. Perhaps Mrs.—the red-headed doctor's wife—queer I can't think of their names—perhaps she sent them. It would be like her."

The nurse's glance wandered, in the faint light, to where a great jar of daffodils stood upon the farther window sill, their heads nodding faintly in the night breeze. Jordan King's card, which had come with them, was tucked away in a drawer near by with two other cards, bearing the same name, which had accompanied other flowers. Miss Arden doubted if her patient realized who had sent any of them. Afterward—if there was to be an afterward—she would show the cards to her. Miss Arden, like many other people, knew Jordan King by reputation, for the family was an old and established one in the city, and the early success of the youngest son in a line not often taken up by the sons of such families was noteworthy. Also he was good to look at, and Miss Arden, experienced nurse though she was and devoted to her profession, had not lost her appreciation of youth and health and good looks in those who were not her patients.

Unexpectedly, at this hour of the night—it was well toward one o'clock—the door suddenly opened very quietly and a familiar big figure entered. Springing up to meet Doctor Burns, Miss Arden showed no surprise. It was a common thing for this man, summoned to the hospital at unholy hours for some critical case, to take time to look in on another patient not technically in need of him.

The head on the pillow turned at the slight sound beside it. Two wide eyes stared up at Burns. "You've made a mistake, I think," said the patient's voice, politely yet firmly. "My doctor has red hair. I know him by that. Your hair is black."

"I presume it is, in this light," responded Burns, sitting down by the bed. "It's pretty red, though, by daylight. In that case will you let me stay a minute?" His fingers pressed the pulse. Then his hand closed over hers with a quieting touch. "Since you're awake," he said, "you may as well have one extra bath to send you back to sleep."

The head on the pillow signified unwillingness. "I'd take one to please my red-headed doctor, but not you."

"You'd do anything for him, eh?" questioned Burns, his eyes on the chart which the nurse had brought him and upon which she was throwing the light of a small flash. "Well, you see he wants you to have this bath; he told me so."

"Very well, then," she said with a sigh. "But I don't like them. They make me shiver."

"I know it. But they're good for you. They keep your red-headed doctor master of the situation. You want him to be that, don't you?"

"He'd be that anyway," said she confidently.

Burns smiled, but the smile faded quickly. He gave a few brief directions, then slipped away as quietly as he had come.

It was well into the next week when one morning he encountered Jordan King, who had been out of town for several days. King came up to him eagerly. Since this meeting occurred just outside the hospital, where Burns's car had been standing in its accustomed place for the last hour, it might not have been a wholly accidental encounter.

King made no attempt to maneuver for information. Maneuvering with Red Pepper Burns, as the young man was well aware, seldom served any purpose but to subject the artful one to a straight exposure. He asked his question abruptly.

"I want to hear how Miss Linton is doing. I'm just back from Washington—haven't heard for a week."

Burns frowned. No physician likes to be questioned about his cases, particularly if they are not progressing to suit him. But he answered, in a sort of growl: "She's not doing."

King looked startled. "You mean—not doing well?"

"She's fighting for existence—and—slipping."

"But—you haven't given her up?"

Burns exploded with instant wrath. King might have known that question would make him explode. "Given her up! Don't you know a red-headed fiend like me better than that?"

"I know you're a bulldog when you get your teeth in," admitted Jordan King, looking decidedly unhappy and anxious. "If I'm just sure you've got 'em in, that's enough."

Burns grunted. The sound was significant.

King ventured one more question, though Red Pepper's foot was on his starter, and the engine had caught the spark and turned over. "If there's anything I could do," he offered hurriedly and earnestly. "Supply a special nurse, or anything—"

Burns shook his head. "Two specials now, and half the staff interested. It's up to Anne Linton and nobody else. If she can do the trick—she and Nature—all right. If not—well—Thanks for letting go the car, Jord. This happens to be my busy day."

Jordan King looked after him, his heart uncomfortably heavy. Then he stepped into his own car and drove away, taking his course down a side street from which he could get a view of certain windows. They were wide open to the May breeze and the sunshine, but no pots of daffodils or other flowers stood on their empty sills. He knew it was useless to send them now.

"But if she does pull through," he said to himself between his teeth, "I'll bring her such an armful of roses she can't see over the top of 'em. God send I get the chance!"

CHAPTER V

Susquehanna

Red Pepper Burns drove into the vine-covered old red barn behind his house which served as his garage, and stopped his engine with an air of finality.

"Johnny," said he, addressing the young man who was accustomed to drive with him—and for him when for any reason he preferred not to drive himself, which was seldom—and who kept the car in the most careful trim, "not for man or beast, angel or devil will I go out again to-night."

Johnny Carruthers grinned. "No, sir," he replied. "Not unless they happen to want you," he added.

"Not if they offer me a thousand dollars for the trip," growled his master.

"You would for a dead beat, though," suggested the devoted servant, who by virtue of five years of service knew whereof he spoke, "if he'd smashed his good-for-nothin' head."

"Not if he'd smashed his whole blamed body—so long as there was another surgeon in the county who could do the job."

"That's just the trouble," argued Johnny. "You'd think there wasn't."

Red Pepper looked at him. "Johnny, you're an idiot!" he informed him. Then he strode away toward the house.

As he went into his office the telephone rang. The office was empty, for it was dinner-time, and Miss Mathewson was having a day off duty on account of her mother's illness. So, unhappily for the person at the other end of the wire, the Doctor himself answered the ring. It had been a hard day, following other hard days, and he was feeling intense fatigue, devastating depression, and that unreasoning irritability which is born of physical weariness and mental unrest.

"Hello," shouted the victim of these disorders into the transmitter. "What?.No, I can'tWhat? No. Get somebody else.What?.I can't, I say.Yes, you can. Plenty of 'em.What?.Absolutely *no*! Good-bye!"

"I ought to feel better after that," muttered Burns, slamming the receiver on the hook. "But somehow I don't."

In two minutes he was splashing in a hot bath, as always at the end of a busy day. From the tub he was summoned to the telephone, the upstairs extension, in his own dressing room. With every red hair erect upon his head after violent towelling, he answered the message which reached his unwilling ears.

"What's that? Worse? She isn't—it's all in her mind. Tell her she's all right. I saw her an hour ago. What?.Well, that's all imagination, as I've told her ten thousand times. There's absolutely nothing the matter with her heart.No, I'm not coming—she's not to be babied like that.No, I won't. Good-bye!"

The door of the room softly opened. A knock had preceded the entrance of Ellen, but Burns hadn't heard it. He eyed her defiantly.

"Do you feel much, much happier now?" she asked with a merry look.

"If I don't it's not the fault of the escape

valve. I pulled it wide open."

"I heard the noise of the escaping steam." She came close and stood beside him, where he sat, half dressed and ruddy in his bathrobe. He put up both arms and held her, lifting his head for her kiss, which he returned with interest.

"That's the first nice thing that's happened to me to-day—since the one I had when I left you this morning," he remarked. "I'm all in to-night, and ugly as a bear, as usual. I feel better, just this minute, with you in my arms and a bath to the good, but I'm a beast just the same, and you'd best take warning.Oh, the—"

For the telephone bell was ringing again. From the way he strode across the floor in his bathrobe and slippers it was small wonder that the walls trembled. His wife, watching him, felt a thrill of sympathy for the unfortunate who was to get the full force of that concussion. With a scowl on his brow he lifted the receiver, and his preliminary "Hello!" was his deepest-throated growl. But then the scene changed. Red Pepper listened, the scowl giving place to an expression of a very different character. He asked a quick question or two, with something like a most unaccustomed breathlessness in his voice, and then he said, in the businesslike but kind way which characterized him when his sympathies were roused:

"I'll be there as quick as I can get there. Call Doctor Buller for me, and let Doctor Grayson know I may want him."

Rushing at the completion of his dressing he gave a hurried explanation, in answer to his wife's anxious inquiry, "It isn't Anne Linton?"

"It's worse, it's Jord King. He's had a bad accident—confound his recklessness! I'm afraid he's made a mess of it this time for fair, though I can't be sure till I get there."

"Where is he?" Ellen's face had turned pale.

"At the hospital. His man Aleck is hurt, too. Call Johnny, please, and have him bring the car around and go with me."

Ellen flew, and five minutes later watched her husband gulp down a cup of the strong coffee Cynthia always made him at such crises when, in spite of fatigue, he must lose no time nor adequately reënforce his physical energy with food.

"Oh, I'm so sorry you couldn't rest to-night," she said as he set down the cup and, pulling his hat over his eyes, picked up the heavy surgical bags.

"Couldn't, anyway, with the universe on my mind, so I might as well keep going," was Burns's gruff reply, though the kiss he left on her lips was a long one and spoke his appreciation of her tender comradeship.

She did not see him again till morning, though she lay awake many hours. He came in at daylight; she heard the car go in at the driveway, and, rising hurriedly, was ready to meet him when he came into the living room downstairs.

"Up so early?" questioned Burns as he saw her. The next minute he had folded her in one of those strong-armed embraces which speak of a glad return to one whose life is a part of one's own. "I wonder," he murmured, with his cheek pressed to hers, "if a man ever came back to sweeter arms than these!"

But she knew, in spite of this greeting, that his heart was heavy. Her own heart sank. But she waited, asking no questions. He would tell her when he was ready.

He drew her down upon the couch beside him and sat with his arm around her. "No, I don't want to lie down just yet," he said. "I just want you. I'm keeping you in suspense, I know; I oughtn't to do that. Jord's life is all right, and he'll be himself again in time, but—well, I've lost my nerve for a bit—I can't talk about it."

His voice broke. By and by it steadied again; and, his weariness partially lifted by the heartening little breakfast Ellen brought him on a tray, he told her the story of the night:

"Jord was coming in from the Coldtown Waterworks, forty miles out, late for dinner and hustling to make up time. Aleck, the Kings' chauffeur, was with him. They were coming in at a good clip, even for a back street, probably twenty-five or thirty. There wasn't much on the street except ahead, by the curb, a wagon, and coming toward him a big motor truck. When he was fifty feet from the wagon a fellow stepped out from behind it to cross the street. It was right under the arc light, and Jord recognized Franz—'Little Hungary' you know—with his fiddle under his arm, crossing to go in at the stage door of the Victoria Theatre, where he plays. The boy didn't see them at all.

"Neither Jord nor Aleck can tell much about it yet, of course, but from the little I got I know as well as if I had been there what happened. He slammed on the brakes—it was the only thing he could do, with the motor truck taking up half the narrow street. The pavement was wet—a shower was just over. Of course she skidded completely around to the left, just missing the truck, and when she hit the curb over she went. She jammed Jord between the car and the ground, injuring his back pretty badly but not permanently, as nearly as I can make out. But she crushed Aleck's right arm so that—"

He drew a long breath, a difficult breath,

and Ellen, listening, cried out against the thing she instantly felt it meant.

"O Red! You don't mean—"

He nodded. "I took it off, an hour afterward—at the shoulder."

Ellen turned white, and in a moment more she was crying softly within the shelter of her husband's arm. He sat with set lips, and eyes staring at the empty fireplace before him. Presently he spoke again, and his voice was very low, as if he could not trust it:

"Aleck was game. He was the gamest chap I ever saw. All he said when I told him was, 'Go ahead, Doctor.' I never did a harder thing in all my life. I suppose army surgeons get more or less used to it, but somehow—when I knew what that arm meant to Aleck, and how an hour before it had been a perfect thing, and now—"

He did not try to tell her more just then, but later, when both were steadied, he added a few more important details to the story:

"Franz went to the hospital with them—

wouldn't leave them—ran the risk of losing his position. Do you know, Jord has been teaching that boy English, evenings, and naturally Franz adores him. I suppose Jord would have taken that skid for any blamed beggar who got in his way, but of course it didn't take any force off the way he jammed on those brakes when he saw it was a friend he was going to hit. And a friend he was going to maim—pretty hard choice to make, wasn't it? But of course it was sure death to Franz if he hit him, at that pace, so there was nothing else to do but take the chance for himself and Aleck. Maybe you can guess, though, how he feels about Aleck. One wouldn't think he knew he'd been cruelly hurt himself."

"Oh! I thought—"

"Jord's back will give him a lot of trouble for a while, but his spine isn't seriously injured, if I know my trade. Altogether—well—the nurses have got a couple of interesting cases on their hands for a while. No doubt Aleck will be well looked after. As for Jord—he'll be so much the more helpless of the two for a while, I'm afraid he'll prove a distraction that will demoralize the force."

He smiled faintly for the first time, but his face sobered again instantly.

"Anne Linton's pretty weak, but she took a little nourishment sanely this morning just before I came away. Miss Arden feels a trifle encouraged. I confess this thing of Jord's has knocked the girl out of my mind for the time being, though I shall get her back again fast enough, if I don't find things going right when I see her. Well"—he turned his wife's face toward him, with a hand against her cheek—"it's all out now, and I'm eased a bit by the telling. I wish I could get forty winks, just to make a break between last night and this morning."

"You shall. Lie down and I'll put you to sleep."

He did not think it possible, in spite of his exhaustion, but presently under her quieting touch he was over the brink, greatly to Ellen's relief. Her heart contracted with love and sympathy as she watched his face. It was a weary face, now in its relaxation, and there were heavy shadows under the closed eyes. Every now and then a frown crossed the broad brow, as if the sleeper were not wholly at ease, could not forget, even in his dreams, what he had had to do a few hours ago. She thought of young Aleck with his manly, smiling face, his pride in keeping Jordan King's car as fine and efficient beneath its hood—mud-splashed though it often was without—as he did the shining limousine he drove for Mrs. Alexander King, Jordan's mother. She thought of what it must be to him now to know that he was maimed for life. As for King himself, she knew him well enough to understand how his own injuries would count for little beside his distress in having had to deal the blow which had crushed that strong young arm of Aleck's. Her heart ached for them both—and even for poor Franz, weeping at having been the innocent cause of all this havoc.

Two hours' sleep did his wife secure for Burns before he woke, stoutly avowing himself fit for anything again, and setting off, immediately breakfast was over, for the place to which his thoughts had leaped with his first return to consciousness.

"Can't rest till I see old Jord. Did I tell you

that he insisted on Aleck's having the room next his, precisely as big and airy as his own? There's a door between, and when it's open they can see each other. When I left Jord the door was open, and he was staring in at Aleck, who was still sleeping off the anesthetic, and a big tear was running down Jord's cheek. He can't stir himself, but that doesn't seem to bother him any. He's going to suffer a lot of pain with his back, but he'll suffer ten times more looking at that bandaged shoulder of Aleck's."

It was four days later that Ellen saw King. She was prepared to find him, as Burns had called him, "game," but she had not known just all that term means among men when it is applied to such a one as he. If he had been receiving her after having suffered a bad wrench of the ankle he could not have treated the occasion more simply.

"This is mighty good of you," he said, reaching up a well-developed right arm from his bed, where he lay flat on his back without so much as a pillow beneath his head. His hair was carefully brushed, his bandages were concealed, his lips were smiling, and altogether he was, except for his prostrate position, no picture of an invalid.

"I've just been waiting to come," she said, returning the firm pressure of his hand with that of both her own.

"And meanwhile you've kept me reminded of you by these wonderful flowers," he said with a nod toward the ranks on ranks of roses which crowded table and window sills.

"Oh, but not all those!" she denied. "I might have known you would be deluged with them. Daisies and buttercups out of the fields would have been better."

"No, because those you sent look like you. Doctor Burns won't grudge me the pleasure of saying now what I like to his wife—and it's the first time I've really dared tell you what I thought."

"What a charming compliment! But I'm going to send you something much more substantial now—good things to eat, and books to read, if I can just find out what you like—and even games to play, if you care for them."

"I'll be delighted, if they're something Aleck and I can play together. You see when that door is open we aren't far apart, and it won't be long, Doctor Burns says, before he'll be walking in here to keep me company—till he gets out."

"He is doing well, I hear. I'm so glad."

"Yes, that husky young constitution of his is telling finely—plus your husband's surgery. My poor boy!" He shut his lips upon the words, and kept them closely pressed together for an instant. "My word, Mrs. Burns—he's the stuff that heroes are made of! His living to earn for the rest of his life—with one arm—and you'd think he'd lost the tip of one finger. If ever I let that boy go out of my employ—why, he's worth more as a shining example of pluck than other men are worth with two good arms!"

"I must go and see him—if he'd care to have me."

"He'd take it as the honour of his life. He's crazy over the flowers you sent him."

"Would he care for books? And what

sort? I'm going to bring both of you books."

"Stories of adventure will suit Aleck—the wilder the better. Odd choice—for such a peaceable-looking fellow, isn't it? As for me—something I'll have to work hard to listen to, something to keep an edge on my mind. I've counted the cracks in the ceiling till I have a map of them by heart. I've worked out a system by which I can drain that ceiling country and raise crops there. There isn't much else in this room that I can count or lay out—worse luck! So I've named all the roses, and have wagers with myself as to which will fade first. I'm betting on Susquehanna, that big red one, to outlast all the rest."

When Red Pepper looked in half an hour later, it was to find the door open between the two rooms, and his wife listening, smiling, to an incident of the night just past, as told by first one patient and then the other. The two young men might have been two comrades lying beside a campfire, so gay was their jesting with each other, so light their treatment of the wakeful hours both had spent.

"No, there's nothing the matter with either of them," observed Burns, looking from one bedside to the other. "Franz is the chap with the heavy heart; these two are just enjoying a summer holiday. But I'm not going to keep the communication open long at a time, as yet."

He went in to see Aleck, closing the door again. When he returned he took up a position at the foot of King's bed, regarding him in silence. Ellen looked up at her husband. There was something in his face which had not been there of late—a curiously bright look, as if a cloud were lifted. She studied him intently, and when he returned the scrutiny she raised her eyebrows in an interrogation. He nodded, smiling quizzically.

"Jord," he said, "if you want to keep your secrets to yourself, beware of letting any woman come within range. My wife has just read me as if I were an open book in large black type."

"Bound in scarlet and gold," added Ellen.

"Tell us, Red. You really have good news?"

"The best. I am pretty confident Anne Linton has turned the corner. I hoped it yesterday, but wasn't sure enough to say so. Did you know that, too?"

"Of course. But you were in small type yesterday. To-day he who runs may read. You would know it yourself, wouldn't you, Jordan?"

The man in the bed studied the man who stood at its foot. The two regarded each other as under peculiar circumstances men do who have a strong bond of affection and confidence between them.

"He's such a bluffer," said King. "I hadn't supposed anybody could tell much about what he was thinking. But I do see he looks pretty jolly this morning, and I don't imagine it's all bluff. I'm certainly glad to hear Miss Linton is doing well."

"Doing well isn't exactly the phrase even now," admitted Red Pepper. "There are lots of things that can happen yet. But the wind and waves have floated her little craft off the rocks, and the leaks in the boat are stopped. If she doesn't spring any more, and the winds continue favourable, we'll make port."

Jordan King looked as happy as if he had been the brother of this patient of Burns's, whom neither of them had known a month ago, and whom one of them had seen but once.

"That's great," he said. "I haven't dared to ask since I came here myself, knowing how poor the prospects were the last time I did ask. I was afraid I should surely hear bad news. When can we begin to send her flowers again? Couldn't I send some of mine? I'd like her to have Susquehanna there, and Rappahannock—and I think Arapahoe and Apache will run them pretty close on lasting. Would you mind taking them to her when you go?" His eyes turned to Mrs. Burns.

"I'd love to, but I shall not dare to tell her you are here, just yet. She is very weak, isn't she, Red?"

"As a starved pussy cat. The flowers won't hurt her, but we don't want to rouse her sympathies as yet."

"I should say not. Don't mention me; just take her the posies," instructed King, his cheek showing a slight access of colour.

"You won't know whether Susquehanna wins your wager or not," Ellen reminded him as she obediently separated the indicated blooms, magnificent great hothouse specimens with stems like pillars. That the finest of all these roses, not excepting those she had sent herself, had come from private greenhouses, she well knew. The Kings lived in the centre of the wealthiest quarter of the city, though not themselves possessed of more than moderate riches. Their name, however, was an old and honoured one, Jordan himself was a favourite, and none in the city was too important to be glad to be admitted at his home.

"Anything more I can do for you before I go?" inquired Burns of his patient when Ellen had gone, smiling back at King from over the big roses and promising to keep track of Susquehanna for him in her daily visits.

"Nothing, thank you. You did it all an hour ago, and left me more comfortable than I expected to be just yet. I'm not sure whether it was the dressing or the visit that did me the most good."

"You're a mighty satisfactory sort of patient. That good clean blood of yours is telling already in your recovery from shock. It tells in another way, too."

"What's that?"

"Sheer pluck."

King's eyelids fell. It meant much to him to stand well in the estimation of this man, himself distinguished for the cool daring of his work, his endurance of the hard drudgery of his profession as well as the brilliant performance on occasion. "I'm glad you think so—Red Pepper Burns," King answered daringly. Then, as the other laughed, he added: "Do you know what would make me the most docile patient you could ask?"

"Docile doesn't seem just the word for you—but I'd be glad to know, in case of emergency."

"Let me call you that—the name your best friends have for you. It's a bully name. I know I'm ten years younger—but—"

"Good lack! Jordan King, call me anything you like! I'll appreciate it."

"You've no idea how long I've wanted to do it—Red," vowed the younger man, with the flush again creeping into his cheek.

"Why didn't you long ago?" Burns demanded. "Surely dignity's no characteristic of mine. If Anne Linton can call me 'Red Head' on no acquaintance at all—"

"She didn't do that!" King looked a little as if he had received a blow.

"Only when she was off her head, of course. She took me for a wildcat once, poor child. No, no—when she was sane she addressed me very properly. She's back on the old decorous ground now. Made me a beautiful little speech this morning, informing me that I had to stop calling her 'little girl,' for she was twenty-four years old. As she looks about fifteen at the present, and a starved little beggar at that, I found it a bit difficult to begin on 'Miss Linton,' particularly as I have been addressing her as 'Little Anne' all the time."

"Starved?" King seemed to have paused at this significant word.

"Oh, we'll soon fill her out again. She's really not half so thin as she might be under the old-style treatment. It strikes me you have a good deal of interest in my patients, Jord. Shall I describe the rest of them for you?"

Burns looked mischievous, but King did not seem at all disturbed.

"Naturally I am interested in a girl you made me bring to the hospital myself. And at present—well—a fellow feeling, you know. I see how it is myself now. I didn't then."

"True enough. Well, I'll bring you daily bulletins from Miss Anne. And when she's strong enough I'll break the news to her of your proximity. Doubtless your respective nurses will spend their time carrying flowers back and forth from one of you to the other."

"More than likely," King admitted. "Anything to fill in the time. I'm sorry I can't take her out in my car when she's ready. I've been thinking, Doctor—Red," he went on hastily, "that there's got to be some way for Aleck to drive that car in the future. I'm going to work out a scheme while I lie here."

"Work out anything. I'll prophesy right now that as soon as you get fairly comfortable you'll think out more stuff while you're lying on your back than you ever did in a given period of time before. It won't be lost time at all; it'll be time gained. And when you do get back on your legs—no, don't ask me when that'll be, I can't tell nor any other fellow—but when you do get back you'll make things fly as they never did before—and that's going some."

"You *are* a great bluffer, but I admit that I like the sound of it," was King's parting speech as he watched Burns depart.

On account of this latest interview he was able to bear up the better under the immediately following visit of his mother, an aristocratic-looking, sweet-faced but sad-eyed lady, who could not yet be reconciled to that which had happened to her son, and who visited him twice daily to bring hampers of fruit, food, and flowers, in quantity sufficient to sustain half the patients in a near-by ward. She invariably shed a few quiet tears over him which she tried vainly to conceal, addressed him in a mournful tone, and in spite of his efforts to cheer her managed to leave behind her after each visit an atmosphere of depression which it took him some time and strength to overcome.

"Poor mother, she can't help it," philosophized her son. "What stumps me, though, is why one who takes life so hard should outlive a man like my father, who was all that is brave and cheerful. Perhaps it took it out of him to be always playing the game boldly against her fears. But even so—give me the bluffers, like Red Pepper—and like Mrs. Red. Jove! but she's a lovely woman. No wonder he adores her. So do I—with his leave. And so does Anne Linton, I should imagine. Poor little girl—what does she look like, I wonder?"

If he could have seen her at that moment, holding Susquehanna against her hollow young cheek, the glowing flower making the white face a pitiful contrast, he would have been even more touched than he could have imagined. Also—he would have felt that his wager concerning Susquehanna was likely to be lost. It is not conducive to the life of a rose to be loved and caressed as this one was being. But since it was the first of her flowers that Anne Linton had been able to take note of and enjoy, it might have been considered a life—and a wager—well lost.

CHAPTER VI

Heavy Local Mails

Anne Linton lifted her head ever so little from the allowed incline of her pillow in the Good Samaritan Hospital. She peered anxiously at the tray being borne toward her by Selina Arden, most scrupulously conscientious of all trained nurses, and never more rigidly exact than when the early diet of patients in convalescence was concerned.

"Is that all?" murmured Anne in a tone of anguish.

"All!" replied Miss Arden firmly. But she smiled, showing her perfect white teeth—and showing also her sympathy by the tone in which she added: "Poor child!"

"Shall I never, never, never," asked the patient, hungrily surveying the tray at close range, "have enough just to dull these pangs a little? Not enough to satisfy me, of course, but just enough to take the edge off?"

"Very soon now," replied Miss Arden cheerily, "you shall have a pretty good-sized portion of beefsteak, juicy and tender, and you shall eat it all up—"

"And leave not a wrack behind," moaned Anne Linton, closing her eyes. "But you are wrong, Miss Arden—I shall not eat it, I shall *gulp* it—the way a dog does. I always wondered why a dog has no manners about eating. I know now. He is so hungry his eyes eat it first, so his mouth has no chance. Well, I'm certainly thankful for the food on this tray. It's awfully good—what there is of it."

She consumed it, making the process as lingering as was consistent with the ravaging appetite which was a real torture. When the last mouthful had vanished she set her eyes upon the clock—the little travelling clock which was Miss Arden's and which had ticked busily and cheerfully through all those days of illness when Anne's eyes had never once lifted to notice the passage of time.

"I was so long about it," said the girl gleefully, "that now it's only two hours and forty minutes to the next refreshment station. I expect I can keep on living till then if I use all my will power."

"And here's something to make you forget how long two hours and forty minutes are."

Miss Arden went to the door and, returning, laid suddenly in Anne's arms a great, fragrant mass of white bloom, at the smell and touch of which she gave a half-smothered cry of rapture, and buried her face in the midst of it. "White lilacs—oh, white lilacs! The dears—the loves! Oh, where *did* they come from?"

"There's a note that came with them," admitted Miss Arden presently, when she had let the question go unanswered for some time, while Anne, seeming to forget that she had asked it, smelled and smelled of the cool white and green branches as if she could never have enough of them. Into her eyes had leaped a strange look, as if some memory were connected with these outdoor flowers which made them different for her from the hothouse blooms, or even from the daffodils and tulips that had alternated with the roses which had come often since her convalescence began.

Anne reached up an eager hand for the note, a look of surprise on her face. Miss Arden, looking back at her, noted how each day was helping to remove the pallor and wanness from that face. At the moment, under the caress of the lilacs and the surprise of the impending note, it was showing once more a decided touch of its former beauty. Also she was wearing a little invalid's wrap of lace and pink silk, given her by Mrs. Burns, and this helped the effect.

Anne unfolded the note. Miss Arden went away with the empty tray, and remained away some time. Miss Arden, as has been said before, was a most remarkable nurse.

The note read thus:

The Next Corridor, 10:30 A.M.

DEAR MISS LINTON:

The time has come, it seems to me,

for two patients who have nothing to do but while away the hours for a bit longer, to help each other out. What do you say? I suppose you don't know that I've been lying flat on my back now for a fortnight, getting over a rather bad spill from my car. I'm pretty comfortable now, thank you, so don't waste a particle of sympathy; but the hours must certainly drag for you as they do for me, and my idea is that we ought to establish some sort of system of intercommunication. I have an awfully obliging nurse, and a young man with a fiddle here besides, and I'd like to send you a short musicale when you feel up to it. Are you fond of music? I have a notion you are. Franz will come and play for you whenever you say. But besides that I'd awfully like to have a note from you as soon as you are able to write. I'll answer it, you know—and then you'll answer that, perhaps—and so the hours will go by. I know this is a rather free-and-easy-sounding proposition from a perfect stranger, as I suppose you think me, but circumstances do alter cases, you know, and if our circumstances can't alter our cases, then it's no good being laid up!

Hearty congratulations on that raging appetite. You see Doctor Burns is good enough to keep me informed as to how you come on. You certainly seem to be coming on now. Please keep it up. I shouldn't dare ask you to write to me if the Doctor hadn't said you could—if you wouldn't do it enough to tire you. So—I'm hoping.

Yours, under the same roof,

JORDAN KING.

"Good morning!" said a beloved voice from the doorway. Anne looked up eagerly from her letter.

"Oh, Mrs. Burns—good morning! And won't you please stand quite still for a minute while I look at you?"

Ellen laughed. To other people than

Anne Linton she was always the embodiment of quiet charm in her freshness of attire and air of general daintiness. In the pale gray and white of her summer clothing, with a spray of purple lilac tucked into her belt, she was a vision to rest the eye upon. "You are looking ever so well yourself to-day," Ellen said as she sat down close beside Anne, facing her. "Another week and you will be showing us what you really look like."

"The little pink cover-up does me as much good as anything," declared Anne. "I never thought I could wear pink with my carroty hair. But Miss Arden says I can wear anything you say I can, and I believe her."

"Your hair is bronze, not carroty, and that apricot shade of pink tones in with it beautifully. What a glorious mass of white lilacs! I never saw any so fine."

"They're wonderful. I insisted on keeping them right here, I'm so fond of the fragrance. They came from Mr. King," said Anne frankly. "And a note from him says he's here in the hospital with an injured back. I'm so sorry. Please tell me how badly he is hurt."

"He will have to be patient for some weeks longer, I believe, but there is no permanent injury. Meanwhile, he is like any man confined, restless for want of occupation. Still, he keeps his time pretty full." And Ellen proceeded to recount the story of Franz, and of how Jordan King was continuing here in the hospital to teach him to speak English, finding him the quickest and most grateful of pupils.

"How splendid of him! He's going to send Franz to play for me. I can't think of anything—except beefsteak—I should like so much!" and Anne laughed, her face all alight with interest. But the next instant it sobered. "Mrs. Burns," she said, "there's something I want to say very much, and so far the Doctor hasn't let me. But I'm quite strong enough now to begin to make plans, and one of them is this: The minute I'm able to leave the hospital I want to go to some inexpensive place where I can stay without bothering anybody. You have all been so wonderful to me I can never express my gratitude, but I'm beginning to feel—oh, can't you guess how anxious I am to be taking care of myself again? And I want you to know that I have quite money enough to do it until I can go on with my work."

Mrs. Burns looked at her. In the excitement of talking the girl's face looked rounder and of a better colour than it had yet shown, and her eyes were glowing, eyes of such beauty as are not often seen. But for all that, she seemed like some lovely child who could no more take care of itself than could a newborn kitten. Ellen laid one hand on hers.

"You are not to think about such things yet, dear," she said. "Do you imagine we have not grown very fond of you, and would let you go off into some place alone before you are fully yourself again? Not a bit of it. As soon as you can leave here you are coming to me as my guest. And when you are playing tennis with Bob, on our lawn, you may begin to talk about plans for the future."

Anne stared back at her, a strange expression on her face. "Oh, no!" she breathed.

"Oh, yes! You can't think how I am looking

forward to it. Meanwhile—you are not to tire yourself with talking. I only stopped for a minute, and the Doctor is waiting by now. Good-bye, my dear." And before Anne could protest she was gone, having learned, by experience, that the way to terminate useless argument with the one who is not strong enough to be allowed to argue is by making early escape.

That afternoon, having recovered from the two surprises of the morning, Anne asked for pencil and paper. Miss Arden, supplying them, stipulated that their use should cover but five minutes.

"It is one of the last things we let patients do," she said, "though it is the thing they all want to do first. There is nothing so tiring as letter writing."

"I'm not going to write a letter," Anne replied, "just a hail to a fellow sufferer. Only I'm no sufferer, and I'm afraid he is."

She wrote her note, and it was presently handed to Jordan King. He had wondered very much what sort of answer he should have, feeling that nothing could reveal the sort of person this girl was so surely as a letter, no matter how short. He had been sure he recognized education in her speech, breeding in her manner, high intelligence as well as beauty in her face, but—well, the letter would reveal. And so it did, though it was written in a rather shaky hand, in pencil, on one of Miss Arden's hospital record blanks—of all things!

Dear Mr. King:

It is the most wonderful thing in the world to be sitting up far enough to be able to write and tell you how sorry I am that you are lying down. But Mrs. Burns assures me that you are fast improving and that soon you will be about again. Meanwhile you are turning your time of waiting to a glorious account in teaching poor Franz to speak English. Surely he must have been longing to speak it, so that he might tell you the things in his heart—about that dreadful night. But I know you don't want me to write of that, and I won't.

Of course I should care to have him play for me, and I hope he may do it soon—to-morrow, perhaps. I wonder if he knows the Schubert "*Frühlingstraum*"—how I should love to hear it! As for your interesting plan for relieving the passing hours, I should hardly be human if I did not respond to it! Only please never write when you don't feel quite like it—and neither will I.

The white lilacs were even more beautiful than the roses and the daffodils. There was a long row of white lilac trees at one side of a garden I used to play in—I shall never, never forget what that fragrance was like after a rain! And now that my sun is shining again—after the rain—you may imagine what those white lilacs breathe of to me.

With the best of good wishes,

Anne Linton.

Jordan King read this note through three times before he folded it back into its original creases. Then he shut it away in a leather-bound writing tablet which lay by his side. "Franz," he said, addressing the youth who was at this hour of the day his sole attendant, "can you play Schubert's '*Frühlingstraum*'?"

He had to repeat this title several times, with varying accents, before he succeeded in making it intelligible. But suddenly Franz leaped to an understanding.

"Yess—yess—yess—yess—sair," he responded joyously, and made a dive for his violin case.

"Softly, Franz," warned his master. As this was a word which had thus far been often used in his education, on account of the fact that the hospital did not belong exclusively to King—strange as that might seem to Franz who worshipped him—it was immediately comprehended. Without raising the tones of his instrument, Franz was able presently to make clear to King that the music he was asked to play was of the best at his command.

"No wonder she likes that," was King's inward comment. "It's a strange, weird thing, yet beautiful in a haunting sort of way, I imagine, to a girl like her, and I don't know but it would be to me if I heard it many times—while I was smelling lilacs in the rain," he added, smiling to himself.

That hint of a garden had rather taken hold of his imagination. More than likely, he said to himself, it had been her own garden—only she would not tell him so lest she seem to try to convey an idea of former prosperity. A different sort of girl would have said "our garden."

Next morning, at the time of Mrs. Burns's visit to the hospital, King sent Franz to play for Miss Linton. With her breakfast tray had come his second note telling her of this intention, so she had two hours of anticipation—a great thing in the life of a convalescent. With every bronze lock in shining order, with the little wrap of apricot pink silk and lace about her shoulders, with an extra pillow at her back, Miss Anne Linton awaited the coming of the "Court Musician," as King had called him.

"It's a very good thing Jord can't see her at this minute," observed Burns to his wife as he met her in the hall outside the door. "The prettiest convalescent has less appeal for a doctor than a young woman of less good looks in strapping health—naturally, for he gets quite enough of illness and the signs thereof. But to a lusty chap like King Miss Anne's present frail appearance would undoubtedly enlist his chivalry. Those are some eyes of hers, eh?"

"I think I have never seen more beautiful eyes," Ellen agreed heartily.

Her husband laughed. "I have," he said, and went his way, having no time for morning musicales.

That afternoon Anne Linton, having had all her pillows removed and having obediently lain still and silent for two long hours, was permitted to sit up again and write a note to King to tell him of the joy of the morning:

> Dear Mr. King:
>
> It was as if the twilight were falling, with the stars coming out one by one. By and by they were all shining, and I was on a mountain top somewhere, with the wind blowing softly against my face. It

was dark and I was all alone, but I didn't mind, for I was strong, strong again, and I knew I could run down by and by and be with people. Then a storm came on, and I lifted my face to if and loved it, and when it died away the stars were shining again between the clouds. Somewhere a little bird was singing—I opened my eyes just there, and your Franz was looking at me and smiling, and I smiled back. He seemed so happy to be making me happy—for he was, of course. After a while it was dawn—the loveliest dawn, all flushed with pink and silver, and I couldn't keep my eyes shut any more for looking at the musician's face. He is a real musician, you know, and the music he makes comes out of his soul.

When it was all over and he and Mrs. Burns were gone, my tray came in. This is a frightful confession, but I am not a real musician; I merely love good music with some sort of understanding of what it means to those who really care, as Franz does. To me, after all

> the emotion, my tray looked like a sort of solid rock that I could cling to. And I had a piece of wonderful beefsteak—ah, now you are laughing! Never mind—I'll show you the two scenes.

Upon the second sheet was something which made Jordan King open his eyes. There were two little drawings—the simplest of pencil sketches, yet executed with a spirit and skill which astonished him. The first was of Franz himself, done in a dozen lines. There was no attempt at a portrait, yet somehow Franz was there, in the very set of the head, the angle of the lifted brow, the pose of the body, most of all in the indication of the smiling mouth, the drooping eyelids. The second picture was a funny sketch of a big-eyed girl devouring food from a tray. Two lines made the pillows behind her, six outlined the tray, a dozen more demonstrated plainly the famishing appetite with which the girl was eating. It was all there—it was astonishing how it was all there.

"My word!" he said as he laid down the

sheets—and took them up again, "that's artist work, whether she knows it or not. She must know it, though, for she must have had training. I wonder where and how."

He called Miss Arden and showed her the sketches.

"Dear me, but they're clever," she said. "They look like a child's work—and yet they aren't."

"I should say not," he declared very positively. "That sort of thing is no child's work. That's what painters do when they're recording an impression, and I've often looked in more wonder at such sketchy outlines than at the finished product. To know how to get that impression on paper so that it's unmistakable—I tell you that's training and nothing else. I don't know enough about it to say it's genius, too, yet I've had an artist friend tell me it cost him more to learn to take the right sort of notes than to enlarge upon those notes afterward."

When he wrote to Anne next morning—he was not venturing to ask more of her than one exchange a day—he told her what he thought about those sketches:

> I've had that sheet pinned up at the foot of my bed ever since it came, and I'm not yet tired of looking at it. You should have seen Franz's face when I showed it to him. "Ze arteeste!" he exclaimed, and laughed, and made eloquent gestures, by means of which I judged he was trying to express you. He looked as if he were trying to impress me with his own hair, his eyes, his cheeks, his hands; but I knew well enough he meant you. I gathered that he had been not ill pleased with his visit to you, for he proposes another; in fact, I think he would enjoy playing for you every day if you should care to hear him so often. He does not much like to perform in the wards, though he does it whenever I suggest it. He has discovered that though they listen respectfully while he plays his own beloved music, mostly they are happier when he gives them a bit of American ragtime, or a popular

> song hit. His distaste for that sort of thing is very funny. One would think he had desecrated his beloved violin when he condescends to it, for afterward he invariably gives it a special polishing with the old silk handkerchief he keeps in the case—and Miss Arden vows he washes his hands, too. Poor Franz! Your real artist has a hard time of it in this prosaic world doesn't he?

The note ended by saying boldly that King would like another sketch sometime, and he even ventured to suggest that he would enjoy seeing a picture of that row of white lilac trees at the edge of the garden where Anne used to play. It was two days before he got this, and meanwhile a box of water colours had come into requisition. When the sheet of heavy paper came to King he lay looking at it with eyes which sparkled.

At first sight it was just a blur of blues and greens, with irregular patches of white, and gay tiny dashes of strong colour, pinks and purples and yellows.

But when, as Anne had bidden him, he held it at arm's length he saw it all—the garden with its box-bordered beds full of tall yellow tulips and pink and white and purple hyacinths—it was easy to see that this was what they were, even from the dots and dashes of colour; the hedge—it was a real hedge of white lilac trees, against a spring sky all scudding clouds of gray. Like the sketch of Franz, its charm lay entirely in suggestion, not in detail, but was none the less real for that.

There was one thing which, to King's observant eyes, stood out plainly from the little wash drawing. This garden was a garden of the rich, not of the poor. Just how he knew it so well he could hardly have told, after all, for there was no hint of house, or wall, or even summer-house, sundial, terrace, or other significant sign. Yet it was there, and he doubted if Anne Linton knew it was there, or meant to have it so. Perhaps it was that lilac hedge which seemed to show so plainly the hand of a gardener in the planting and tending. The question was—was it her own garden in which she had played, or the garden of her father's employer? Had her father been that gardener, perchance? King instantly rejected this possibility.

CHAPTER VII

White Lilacs

Burns, coming in to see King one day when the exchange of letters had been going on for nearly a fortnight, announced that he might soon be moved to his own home.

King stared at him. "I'm not absolutely certain that I want to go till I can get about on my own feet," he said slowly.

Burns nodded. "I know, but that will be some time yet, and your mother—well, I've put her off as long as I could, but without lying to her I can't say it would hurt you now to be taken home. And lying's not my long suit."

"Of course not. And I suppose I ought to go; it would be a comfort to my mother. But—"

He set his lips and gave no further hint of his unwillingness to go where he would be at the mercy of the maternal fondness which would overwhelm him with the attentions he did not want. Besides—there was another reason why, since he must for the present be confined somewhere, he was loath to leave the friendly walls where there was now so much of interest happening every day. Could he keep it happening at home? Not without much difficulty, as he well foresaw.

"Miss Linton's coming to us on Saturday," observed Burns carelessly, strolling to the window with his hands in his pockets.

"Is she? I didn't suppose she'd be strong enough just yet." King tried to speak with equal carelessness, but the truth was that, with his life bound, as it was at present, within the confines of this room, the incidents of each day loomed large.

"She's gaining remarkably fast. For all her apparent delicacy of constitution when she came to us, I'm beginning to suspect that she's the fortunate possessor of a good deal of vigour at the normal. She says herself she was never ill before, and that's why she didn't give up sooner—couldn't believe there was anything the matter. We can't make her agree to stay with us a day longer than I say is a necessity for safety."

"Where does she want to go? Not back to that infernal book-agenting?" There was a frown between King's well-marked brows.

"Yes, I imagine that's what she intends. She's a very decided young person, and there's not much use telling her what she must and must not do. As for the book itself, it's pretty clever, my wife and Miss Mathewson insist. They say the youngsters of the neighbourhood are crazy over it. Bob knows it by heart, and even the Little-Un studies the pictures half an hour at a time. If children were her buyers she'd have no trouble."

"Have a look at those, will you?"

King reached for a leather writing case on the table at his elbow, took out a pile of sheets, and began to hand them over one by one to Burns.

"What's this? Hullo! Do you mean to say she did this? Well, I like her impudence!"

"So do I," laughed King, looking past Burns's shoulder at a saucy sketch of the big Doctor himself evidently laying down the law about something, by every vigorous line of protest in his attitude and the thrust of his chin. Underneath was written: "Absolutely not! Haven't I said so a thousand times?"

"'Wad some power—'" murmured Burns. "Well, she seems to have the 'power.' I am rather a thunderer, I suppose. What's this next? My wife! Jolly! that's splendid. Hasn't she caught a graceful pose though? Ellen's to the life. Selina Arden? That's good—that's very good. There's your conscientious nurse for you. And this, of herself? Ha! She hasn't flattered herself any. She may have looked like that at one time, but not now—hardly."

"She's looking pretty well again, is she?"

"Both pretty and well. We don't starve our patients on an exclusively liquid diet the way we used to, and they don't come out of typhoid looking half so badly in consequence. And she's been rounding out every day for the last two weeks in fine shape. She's a great little girl, and as full of spirit as a gray squirrel. I'm beginning to believe she's a bit older than I would believe at first; that mind of hers is no schoolgirl's; it's pretty mature. She says frankly she's twenty-four, though she doesn't look over nineteen."

"Is there any reason why I can't see her for a bit of a visit if she goes Saturday?" asked King straightforwardly. It was always a characteristic of his to go straight to a point in any matter; intrigue and diplomacy were not for him in affairs which concerned a girl any more than in those which pertained to his profession. "You see we've been entertaining each other with letters and things, and it would seem a pity not to meet—especially if she'll be leaving town before I'm about."

There was a curiously wistful look in his face as he said this, which Burns understood. All along King had said almost nothing about the torture his present helplessness was to him, but his friend knew.

"Of course she'll come; we'll see to that. She's walking about a little now, and by Saturday she can come down this corridor on her two small feet."

"See here—couldn't I sit up a bit to meet her?"

"Not a sixteenth of a degree. You'll lie exactly as flat as you are now. If it's any consolation I'll tell you that you look like a prostrate man-angel seven feet long."

"Thanks. I'd fire a pillow at you if I had one. I don't want to look like an object for sympathy, that's all."

Burns nodded understandingly. "Well, Jord," he said a moment later, "will you go home on Saturday, too?"

The two looked at each other. Then, "If you say so," King agreed.

"All right. Then we'll get rid of two of our most interesting patients on that happy day. Never mind—the mails will still carry—and Franz is a faithful messenger. What's that, Miss Dwight? All right, I'll be there." And he went out, with a gay nod and wave of the hand to the man on the bed.

This was on Monday. On Tuesday King offered his petition that Anne Linton would pay him a visit before she left on Saturday. When the answer came it warmed his heart more than anything he had yet had from her:

Of course I will come—only I want you to know that I shall be dreadfully sorry to come walking, when you must still lie so long on that poor back. Doctor Burns has told me how brave you are, with all the pain you are still suffering. But I am wonderfully glad to learn that he is so confident of your complete recovery. Just to know that you can be your active self again is wonderful when one thinks what might have happened. I shall always remember you as you seemed to me the day you brought me here. I was, of course, feeling pretty limp, and the sight of you, in such splendid vigour, made me intensely envious. And even though I see you now "unhorsed," I shall not lose my first impression, because I know that by and by you will be just like that again—looking and feeling as if you were fit to conquer the world.

It was the most personal note he had had from her, and he liked it very much. He couldn't help hoping for more next day, and did his best to secure it by the words he wrote in reply. But Wednesday's missive was merely a merrily piquant description of the way she was trying her returning strength by one expedition after another about her room. On Thursday she sent him some very jolly sketches of her "packing up," and on Friday she wrote hurriedly to say that she couldn't write, because she was making little visits to other patients.

Jordan King had never been more exacting as to his dressing than on that Saturday. He studied his face in the glass after an orderly had shaved him, to make sure that the blue bloom it took but a few hours to acquire had been properly subdued. He insisted on a particular silk shirt to wear under the loose black-silk lounging robe which enveloped him, and in which he was to be allowed to-day to lie upon the bed instead of in it. His hair had to be brushed and parted three separate times before he was satisfied.

"I didn't know I was such a fop," he said, laughing, as Miss Dwight rallied him on his preparations for receiving the ladies. "But somehow it seems to make a difference when a man lies on his back. They have him at a disadvantage. Now if you'll just give me a perfectly good handkerchief I'll consider that the reception committee is ready. Thank you. It must be almost time for them, isn't it?"

For a young man who usually spent comparatively little of his time in attentions to members of the other sex, but who was accustomed, nevertheless, to be entirely at his ease with them, King acknowledged to himself that he felt a curious excitement mounting in his veins as the light footsteps of his guests approached.

Mrs. Burns came first into his line of vision, wearing white from head to foot, for it was early June and the weather had grown suddenly to be like that of midsummer. Behind her followed not the black figure King's memory had persistently pictured, but one also clad in white—the very simple white of a plain linen suit, with a close little white hat drawn over the bronze-red hair. Under this hat the eyes King remembered glowed warmly, and now there was health in the face, which was so much more charming than the one he recalled that for a moment he could hardly believe the two the same. Yet—the profile, as she looked at Mrs. Burns, who spoke first, was the one which had been stamped on his mind as one not to be forgotten.

She was looking at him now, and there was no pity in her bright glance—he could not have borne to see it if it had been there. She came straight up to the bed, her hand outstretched—her gloves were in the other, as if she were on her way downstairs, as he presently found she was. She spoke in a full, rich voice, very different from the weary one he had heard before.

"Do you know me?" she asked, smiling.

"Almost I don't. Have you really been ill, or did you make it all up?"

"I'm beginning to believe I did. I feel myself as if it must be all dream. How glad I am to find you able to be dressed. Doctor Burns says you will go home to-day, too."

"This evening, I believe. I thought you were not going till then either."

"This very hour." She glanced at Mrs. Burns. "My good fairy begged that I might go early, because it is her little son's birthday. I am to be at a real party; think of that!"

"The Little-Un's or Bob's?" King asked his other visitor.

Bob was an adopted child, taken by Burns before his marriage, but the little Chester's parents made no difference between them, and a birthday celebration for the older boy was sure to be quite as much of an occasion as for the two-year-old.

"Bob's," Mrs. Burns explained. "He is ten; we can't believe it. And he has set his heart on having Miss Linton at home for his party. He has read her little book almost out of its covers, and she has been doing some place-cards for his guests—the prettiest things!" Ellen opened a small package she was carrying and showed King the cards.

He gazed at them approvingly. "They're the jolliest I ever saw; the youngsters will be crazy over them. For a convalescent it strikes me Miss Linton has been the busiest known to the hospital."

"You, yourself, have kept me rather busy, Mr. King," the girl observed.

"So I have. I'm wondering what I'm to do when you are at Doctor Burns's and I at home."

She smiled. "I shall be there only a week if I keep on gaining as fast as I am now."

"A fortnight," interpolated Mrs. Burns, "is the earliest possible date of your leaving us. And not then unless we think you fit."

"Did you ever know of such kindness?" Anne Linton asked softly of King. "To a perfect stranger?"

He nodded. "Nothing you could tell me

of their kindness could surprise me. About that fortnight—would it be asking a great deal of you to keep on sending me that daily note?"

"Isn't there a telephone in your own room at home?" she asked.

"Yes—how did you know?"

"I guessed it. Wouldn't a little telephone talk do quite as well—or better—than a letter?"

"It would be very nice," admitted King. "But I should hate to do without the letter. The days are each a month long at present, you know, and each hour is equal to twenty-four. Make it a letter, too, will you, please?"

Miss Linton looked at Mrs. Burns. "Do you think circumstances still alter cases?" she inquired.

Her profile, as King caught it again, struck him as a perfect outline. To think of this girl starting out again, travelling alone, selling books from door to door!

"I think you will be quite warranted in being very good to Mr. King—while his hours drag as he describes," Ellen assented cordially.

"As soon as I can sit up at any sort of decent angle I can do a lot of work on paper," King asserted. "Then I'll make the time fly. Meanwhile—it's all right."

They talked together for a little, then King sent for Franz, who came and played superbly, his eager eyes oftenest on Jordan King, like those of an adoring and highly intelligent dog. Anne watched Franz, and King watched Anne. Mrs. Burns, seeming to watch nobody, noted with affectionate and somewhat concerned interest the apparent trend of the whole situation. She could not help thinking, rather dubiously, of Mrs. Alexander King, Jordan's mother.

And, as things happen, it was just as Franz laid down his bow, after a brilliant rendering of a great concerto, that Mrs. Alexander King came in. She entered noiselessly, a slender, tall, black-veiled figure, as scrupulously attired in her conventional deep mourning as if it were not hot June weather, when some lightening of her sombre garb would have seemed not only rational but kind to those who must observe her.

"Oh, mother!" King exclaimed. "In all this heat? I didn't expect you. I'm afraid you ought not to have come."

She bent over him. "The heat has nothing to do with my feelings toward my son. I couldn't neglect you, dear."

She greeted Ellen cordially, who presented Miss Linton. King lost nothing of his mother's polite scrutiny of the girl, who bore it without the slightest sign of recognizing it beyond the lowering of her lashes after the first long look of the tall lady had continued a trifle beyond the usual limit. Book agent though she might be, Miss Linton's manner was faultless, a fact King noted with curious pride in his new friend—whom, though he himself was meeting her for but the second time, he somehow wanted to stand any social test which might be put upon her. And he well knew that his lady mother could apply such tests if anybody could.

In his heart he was saying that it seemed hard luck, he must say good-bye to Anne Linton in that mother's presence. There was small chance to make it a leave-taking of even ordinary good fellowship beneath that dignified, quietly appraising eye, to say nothing of endowing it with a quality which should in some measure compensate for the fact that it might be a parting for a long time to come. However much or little the exchange of notes during these last weeks might have come to mean to Jordan King, aside from the diversion they had offered to one sorely oppressed of mind and body, he resented being now forced to those restrained phrases of farewell which he well knew were the only ones that would commend him to his mother's approval.

Mrs. Burns and Miss Linton rose to go, summoned by Red Pepper himself, who was to take them. In the momentary surge of greeting and small talk which ensued, King surreptitiously beckoned Anne near. He looked up with the direct gaze of the man who intends to make the most of the little that Fate sends him.

"Letters are interesting things, aren't they?" he asked.

"Very. And when they are written by a man lying on his back, who doesn't know when he is down, they are stimulating things," she answered; and there was that in the low tone of her voice and the look of her eyes which was as if she had pinned a medal for gallantry on the breast of the black silk robe.

Mrs. Alexander King looked at her son—and moved nearer. She addressed Anne. "I am more than glad to see, Miss Linton," said she, "that you are fully recovered. Please let me wish you much success in your work. I suppose we shall not see you again after you leave Mrs. Burns."

"No, Mrs. King," responded Anne's voice composedly. "Thank you for that very kind wish."

She turned to the prostrate one once more. She put her hand in his, and he held it fast for an instant, and, in spite of his mother's gaze, it was an appreciable instant longer than formality called for.

"I shall hope to see you again," he said distinctly, and the usual phrase acquired a meaning it does not always possess.

Then they were gone, and he had only the remembrance of Anne's parting look, veiled and maidenly, but the comprehending look of a real friend none the less.

"My dear boy, you must be quite worn out with all this company in this exhausting weather," murmured Mrs. King, laying a cool hand on a decidedly hot brow.

The brow moved beneath her hand, on account of a contraction of the smooth forehead, as if with pain. "I really hadn't noticed the weather, mother," replied her son's voice with some constraint in it.

"You must rest now, dear. People who are perfectly well themselves are often most inconsiderate of an invalid, quite without intention, of course."

"If I never receive any less consideration than I have had here, I shall do very well for the rest of my life."

"I know; they have all been very kind. But I shall be so relieved when I can have you at home, where you will not feel obliged to have other patients on your mind. In your condition it is too much to expect."

Jordan King was a good son, and he loved his mother deeply. But there were moments when, as now, if he could have laid a kind but firm hand upon her handsome, emotional mouth, he would have been delighted to do so.

CHAPTER VIII

Expert Diagnosis

"What would you give for a drive with me this morning?" Burns surveyed his patient, now dressed and downstairs upon a pillared rear porch, wistfulness in his eyes but determination on his lips.

"Do you mean it?"

"Yes. We may as well try what that back will stand. Most of the drive will be sitting still in front of houses, anyhow, and in your plaster jacket you're pretty safe from injury."

"Thank heaven!" murmured Jordan King fervently.

Two minutes later he was beside Burns in the Doctor's car, staring eagerly ahead, lifting his hat now and then as some one gave him interested greeting from passing motor. More than once Burns was obliged to bring his car to a short standstill, so that some delighted friend might grasp King's hand and tell him how good it seemed to see him out. With one and all the young man was very blithe, though he let them do most of the talking. They all told him heartily that he was looking wonderfully well, while they ignored with the understanding of the intelligent certain signs which spoke of physical and mental strain.

"Your friends," Burns remarked as they went on after one particularly pleasant encounter, "seem to belong to the class who possess brains. I wish it were a larger class. Every day I find some patient suffering from depression caused by fool comments from some well-meaning acquaintance."

"I've had a few of those, too," King acknowledged.

"I'll wager you have. Well, among a certain class of people there seems to be an idea that you can't show real sympathy without telling the victim that he's looking very ill, and that you have known several such cases which didn't recover. I have one little woman on my list who would have been well long ago if she hadn't had so many loving friends to impress her with the idea that her case was desperate. I talk Dutch to such people now and then, when I get the chance, but it doesn't do much good. Sometimes I get so thundering mad I can't stand it, and then I rip out something that makes me a lasting enemy."

"You get some comfort out of the explosion, anyhow," King commented, with a glance at the strong profile beside him. "Besides, you may do more good than you know. Anybody who had had a good dressing down from you once wouldn't be likely to forget it in a hurry."

Burns laughed at this, as they stopped in front of a house. King had a half-hour wait while his friend was inside. The car stood in heavy shade, and he was very comfortable. He took a letter from his pocket as he sat, a letter which looked as if it had been many times unfolded, and read it once more, his face very sober as his eyes followed the familiar lines:

Dear Mr. King:

I was very, very sorry to go away

without seeing you to say good-bye after our interesting correspondence. Mrs. Burns and I had such a pleasant visit with your mother, in your absence, that we felt rewarded for our call, and it was good to know that you could be out, yet of course we were very disappointed. I do hope that all will go well with you, and that very rapidly, for I can guess how eager you are to be at work.

Of course once I am off on my travels I shall have no time for letters. No, that isn't quite frank, is it? Well, I will be truthful and say honestly that I am sure it is not best that I should keep on writing. I am glad if the letters have, as you say, helped you through the worst of the siege; they surely have helped me. But now—our ways part. Sometime I may give you a hail from somewhere—when I am lonely and longing to know how you get on. And sometime I may be back at my old home. But wherever I am I shall never forget you, Jordan King, for you have put something into my life which was not there before and I am the better for it. As for you—your life will not be one whit the less big and efficient for this trying experience; it will be bigger, I think, and finer. I am glad, glad I have known you.

Anne Linton.

For the hundredth time King felt his heart sink as he thought of that prevented last interview. His mother had prevented it. It was perfectly true that he was out, and away from home—out in a wheeled chair, which had been pushed by Franz through a gap in the hedge between the Kings' lawn and the Wentworths' next door. Just on the other side of that hedge the chair had paused, where Sally Wentworth, his friend of long standing, was serving tea to a little group of young people, all intimates and all delighted to have the invalid once more in their midst. Under the group of great copper beeches which made of that corner of the Wentworth lawn a summer drawing room, King had sat in his chair drinking tea and listening to gay chatter—and wondering why he had not been able to get Anne Linton on the telephone so far that day. And at that very time, so he now bitterly reflected, she and Mrs. Burns had made their call upon him, only to be told by Mrs. King that he was "out."

His mother was unquestionably a lady, and she had told the truth; he could not conceive of her doing otherwise. He knew that she undoubtedly, quite as Anne had said, had made the call a pleasant one. But she had known that he was within a stone's throw of the house, and that he would be bitterly disappointed not to be summoned. She had not mentioned to him the fact of the call at all until next day—when Anne Linton had been gone a full two hours upon her train. Then, when he had called up Mrs. Burns, in a fever of haste to learn what had happened and what there might yet be a chance of happening, he had discovered that Ellen herself had tried three times to get him, upon the telephone, and had at last realized—though this she did not say—that it was not intended that she should.

King understood his mother perfectly. She would scorn directly to deceive him, yet to intrigue quietly but effectively against him in such a case as this she would consider only her duty. She had seen clearly his interest in the stranger, unintroduced and unvouched for, taken in by kind people in an emergency, and though showing unquestionable marks of breeding, none the less a stranger. She had feared for him, in his present vulnerable condition; and she had done her part in preventing that final parting which might have contained elements of danger. That was all there was to it.

For the present King was helpless, and there could be no possible use in reproaching his mother for her action—or lack of action. Once let him get up on his feet, his own master once more—then it would be of use to talk. And talk he would some day. Also he would act. Meanwhile—

Red Pepper Burns came out of the house and scrutinized his friend and patient closely as he approached. "Want to go on, or shall I take you home?" he inquired.

"Take me on—anywhere—everywhere! Something inside will break loose if you don't." King spoke with a smothered note of irritation new to him in Burns's experience.

"You've about reached the limit, have you?" The question was straightforward, matter-of-fact in tone, but King knew the sympathy behind it.

"I rather have," the young man admitted. "I'm ashamed to own it."

"You needn't be. It's a wonder you haven't reached it sooner; I should have. Well, if you stand this drive pretty well to-day you ought to come on fast. With that back, you may be thankful you're getting off as easily as you are."

"I am thankful—everlastingly thankful. It's just—"

"I know. Blow off some of that steam; it won't hurt you. Here we are on the straight road. I'll open up and give you a taste of what poor Henley felt the first time his crippled body and his big, uncrippled spirit tasted the delight of 'Speed.' Remember?"

"Indeed I do. Oh, I'm not complaining. You understand that, Red?"

"Of course I understand—absolutely. And I understand that you need just what I say—to blow off a lot of steam. Hurt you or not, I'm going to let loose for a couple of miles and blow it off for you."

In silence, broken only by the low song of the motor as it voiced its joy in the widening license to show its power, the two men took the wind in their faces as the car shot down the road, at the moment a clear highway for them. King had snatched off his hat, and his dark hair blew wildly about his forehead, while his eyes watched the way as intently as if he had been driving himself, though his body hardly tensed, so complete was his confidence in the steady hands on the wheel. Faster and faster flew the car, until the speed indicator touched a mark seldom passed by King himself at his most reckless moments. His lips, set at first, broke into a smile as the pointing needle circled the dial, and his eyes, if any could have seen them, would have told the relief there was for him in escape by flight, though only temporary, from the grinding pull of monotony and disablement.

At the turn ahead appeared obstruction, and Burns was obliged to begin slowing down. When the car was again at its ordinary by no means slow pace, King spoke:

"Bless you for a mind reader! That was bully, and blew away a lot of distemper. If you'll just do it again going back I'll submit to the afternoon of a clam in a bed of mud."

"Good. We'll beat that record going back, if we break the speedometer. Racing with time isn't supposed to be the game for a convalescent, but I'm inclined to think it's the dose you need, just the same. I expect, Jord, that the first time you pull on a pair of rubber boots and go to climbing around a big concrete dam somewhere your heart will break for joy."

"My heart will stand anything, so that it's action."

"Will it? I thought it might be a bit damaged. It's had a good deal of reaction to stand lately, I'm afraid."

There was silence for a minute, then King spoke:

"Red, you're a wizard."

"Not much of a one. It doesn't take extraordinary powers of penetration to guess that a flame applied to a bundle of kindling will cause a fire. And when you keep piling on the fuel something's likely to get burned."

"Did I pile on the fuel?"

"You sure did. If there had been gunpowder under the kindling you could have expected an explosion—and a wreck."

"There's no wreck."

"No? I thought there might be—somewhere."

King spoke quickly. "Do you think I carried it too far?"

"I think you carried it some distance—

for an invalid's diversion."

The young man flushed hotly. "I was genuinely interested and I saw no harm. If there's any harm done it's to myself, and I can stand that. I'm not conceited enough to imagine that a broken-backed cripple could make any lasting impression."

Burns turned and surveyed his companion with some amusement. "Do you consider that a description of yourself?"

"I certainly do." Jordan King's strong young jaw took on a grim expression.

"Know this then"—Burns spoke deliberately—"there's not a sane girl who liked you well enough before your accident to marry you who wouldn't marry you now."

"That's absurd. Women want men, not cripples."

"You're no cripple. Stop using that term."

"What else? A man condemned to wear a plaster jacket for at least a year." King evidently did his best not to speak bitterly.

"Bosh! Suppose the same thing happened to me. Would you look on me askance for the rest of my days, no matter what man's job I kept on tackling? Besides, the plaster jacket's only a precaution. You wouldn't disintegrate without it."

King looked at Red Pepper Burns and smiled in spite of himself. "I'm glad to hear that, I'm sure. As for looking at you askance—you are you, R.P. Burns."

"Apply the same logic to yourself. You are you, and will continue to be you, plus some assets you haven't had occasion to acquire before in the way of dogged endurance, control of mind, and such-like qualities, bred of need for them. You will be more to us all than you ever were, and that's saying something. And the back's going to be a perfectly good back; give it time. As for—if you don't mind my saying it—that invalid's diversion, I don't suppose it's hurt you any. What I'm concerned for is the hurt it may have done somebody else. I don't need to tell you that it wasn't possible for Ellen and me to have that little girl on our hearts all that time and not get mightily interested in her. She's the real thing, too, we're convinced, and we care a good deal what happens to her next."

Jordan King drew a deep breath. "So do I."

Burns gave him a quick look. "That's good. But you let her go away without making sure of keeping any hold on her. You don't know where she is now."

King shot him a return look. "That wasn't my fault. That was hard luck."

"I don't think much of luck. Get around it."

"I'll do my best, I promise you. But I wish you'd tell me—"

"Yes?"

"—why you should think I had done her any harm. Heaven knows I wouldn't do that for my right arm!"

"She didn't make a sign—not one—of any

injury, I assure you. She's a gallant little person, if ever there was one—and a thoroughbred, though she may be as poor as a church mouse. No, I should never have guessed it. She went away with all sails set and the flags flying. All I know is what my wife says."

"Please tell me."

"I'm not sure it will be good for you." Burns smiled as he drew up beside a house. "However—if you will have it—she says Miss Anne Linton took away with her every one of your numerous letters, notes, and even calling cards which had been sent with flowers. She also took a halftone snapshot of you out at the Coldtown dam, cut from a newspaper, published the Sunday after your accident. The sun was in your eyes and you were scowling like a fiend; it was the worst picture of you conceivable."

"Girls do those things, I suppose," murmured King with a rising colour.

"Granted. And now and then one does it for a purpose which we won't consider. But a girl of the type we feel sure Miss Linton to be carefully destroys all such things from men she doesn't care for—particularly if she has started on a trip and is travelling light. Of course she may have fooled us all and be the cleverest little adventuress ever heard of. But I'd stake a good deal on Ellen's judgment. Women don't fool women much, you know, whatever they do with men."

He disappeared into a small brown house, and King was left once more with his own thoughts. When Burns came out they drove on again with little attempt at conversation, for Burns's calls were not far apart. King presently began to find himself growing weary, and sat very quietly in his seat during the Doctor's absences, experiencing, as he had done many times of late, a sense of intense contempt for himself because of his own physical weakness. In all his sturdy life he had never known what it was to feel not up to doing whatever there might be to be done. Fatigue he had known, the healthy and not unpleasant fatigue which follows vigorous and prolonged labour, but never weakness or pain, either of body or of mind. Now he was suffering both.

"Had about enough?" Burns inquired as

he returned to the car for the eighth time. "Shall I take you home?"

"I'm all right."

Burns gave him a sharp glance. "To be sure you are. But we'll go home nevertheless. The rest of my work is at the hospital anyhow."

As they were approaching the long stretch of straight road to which King had looked forward an hour ago, but which he was disgusted to find himself actually rather dreading now, a great closed car of luxurious type, and bearing upon its top considerable travelling luggage, slowed down as it neared, and a liveried chauffeur held up a detaining hand. Burns stopped to answer a series of questions as to the best route toward a neighbouring city. There were matters of road mending and detours to be made plain to the inquirers, so the detention occupied a full five minutes, during which the chauffeur got down and came to Burns's side with a road map, with which the two wrestled after the fashion usually made necessary by such aids to travel.

During this period Jordan King underwent a disturbing experience. Looking up with his usual keen glance, one trained to observe whatever might be before it, he took in at a sweep the nature of the party in the big car. That it was a rich man's car, and that its occupants were those who naturally belonged in it, there was no question. From the owner himself, an aristocrat who looked the part, as not all aristocrats do, to those who were presumably his wife, his son, and daughters, all were of the same type. Simply dressed as if for a long journey, they yet diffused that aroma of luxury which cannot be concealed.

The presumable son, a tall, hawk-nosed young man who sat beside the chauffeur, turned to speak to those inside, and King's glance followed his. He thus caught sight of a profile next the open window and close by him. He stared at it, his heart suddenly standing still. Who was this girl with the bronze-red hair, the perfect outline of nose and mouth and chin, the sea-shell colouring? Even as he stared she turned her head, and her eyes looked straight into his.

He had seen Miss Anne Linton only twice, and on the two occasions she had seemed to him like two entirely different girls. But this girl—was she not that one who had come to visit him in his room at the hospital, full of returning health and therefore of waxing beauty and vigour?

For one instant he was sure it was she, no matter how strange it was that she should be here, in this rich man's car—unless—But he had no time to think it out before he was overwhelmed by the indubitable evidence that, whoever this girl was, she did not know him. Her eyes—apparently the same wonderful eyes which he could now never forget—looked into his without a sign of recognition, and her colour—the colour of radiantly blooming youth—did not change perceptibly under his gaze. And after that one glance, in which she seemed to survey him closely, after the manner of girls, as if he were an interesting specimen, her eyes travelled to Red Pepper Burns and rested lightly on him, as if he, too, were a person of but passing significance to the motor traveller looking for diversion after many dusty miles of more or less monotonous sights.

King continued to gaze at her with a steadiness somewhat indefensible except as one considers that all motorists, meeting on the highway, are accustomed to take note of one another as comrades of the road. He was not conscious that the other young people in the car also regarded him with eyes of interest, and if he had he would not have realized just why. His handsome, alert face, its outlines slightly sharpened by his late experiences, his well-dressed, stalwart figure, carried no hint of the odious plaster jacket which to his own thinking put him outside the pale of interest for any one.

But it could not be Anne Linton; of course it could not! What should a poor little book agent be doing here in a rich man's car—unless she were in his employ? And somehow the fact that this girl was not in any man's employ was established by the manner in which the young man on the front seat spoke to her, as he now did, plainly heard by King. Though all he said was some laughing, more or less witty thing about this being the nineteenth time, by actual count since breakfast, that a question of roads and routes had arisen, he spoke as to an equal in social status, and also—this was plainer yet—as to one on whom he had a more than ordinary claim. And King listened for her answer—surely he would know her voice if she spoke? One may distrust the evidence of one's eyes when it comes to a matter of identity, but one's ears are not to be deceived.

But King's ears, stretched though they might be, metaphorically speaking, like those of a mule, to catch the sound of that voice, caught nothing. She replied to the young man on the front seat only by a nod and a smile. Then, as the chauffeur began to fold up his road map, thanking Burns for his careful directions, and both cars were on the point of starting, the object of King's heart-arresting scrutiny looked at him once again. Her straight gaze, out of such eyes as he had never seen but on those two occasions, met his without flinching—a long, steady, level look, which lasted until, under Burns's impatient hand, the smaller car got under motion and began to move. Even then, though she had to turn her head a little, she let him hold her gaze—as, of course, he was nothing loath to do, being intensely and increasingly stirred by the encounter with its baffling hint of mystery. Indeed, she let him hold that gaze until it was not possible for her longer to maintain her share of the exchange without twisting about in the car. As for King, he did not scruple to twist, as far as his back would let him, until he had lost those eyes from his view.

CHAPTER IX

Jordan is a Man

When King turned back again to face the front his heart was thumping prodigiously. Almost he was certain it had been Anne Linton; yet the explanation—if there were one—was not to be imagined. And if it had been Anne Linton, why should she have refused to know him? There could have been little difficulty for her in identifying him, even though she had seen him last lying flat on his back on a hospital bed. And if there had been a chance of her not knowing him—there was Red Pepper.

It was Anne. It could not be Anne. Between these two convictions King's head was whirling. Whoever it was, she had dared to look straight into his eyes in broad daylight at a distance of not more than four feet. He had seen into the very depths of her own bewildering beauty, and the encounter, always supposing her to be the person of whom he had thought continuously for four months, was a thing to keep him thinking about her whether he would or no.

"Anything wrong?" asked Burns's voice in its coolest tones. "I suspect I was something of an idiot to give you such a big dose of this at the first trial."

"I'm all right, thank you." And King sat up very straight in the car to prove it. Nevertheless, when he was at home again he was not sorry to be peremptorily ordered to lie supine on his back for at least three hours.

It was not long after this that King was able to bring about the thing he most desired—a talk with Mrs. Burns. She came to see him one July day, at his request, at an hour when he knew his mother must be away. With her he went straight to his point; the moment the first greetings were over and he had been congratulated on his ability to spend a few hours each day at his desk, he began upon the subject uppermost in his thoughts. He told her the story of his encounter with the girl in the car, and asked her if she thought it could have been Miss Linton.

She looked at him musingly. "Do you

prefer to think it was or was not?" she asked.

"Are you going to answer accordingly?"

"Not at all. I was wondering which I wanted to think myself. I wish I had been with you. I should have known."

"Would you?" King spoke eagerly. "Would you mind telling me how?"

"I can't tell you how. Of course I came to know her looks much better than you; it really isn't strange that after seeing her only twice you couldn't be sure. I don't think any change of dress or environment could have hidden her from me. The question is, of course, why—if it was she—she should have chosen not to seem to know you—unless—"

"Yes—"

She looked straight at him. "Unless—she is not the poor girl she seemed to be. And that explanation doesn't appeal to me. I have known of poor girls pretending to be rich, but I have never, outside of a sensational novel, known a rich girl to pretend to be poor, unless for a visit to a poor quarter for charitable purposes. What possible object could there be in a girl's going about selling books unless she needed to do it? And she allowed me—" She stopped, shaking her head. "No, Jordan, that was not our little friend—or if it was, she was in that car by some curious chance, not because she belonged there."

"So you're going on trusting her?" was King's abstract of these reflections. He scanned her closely.

She nodded. "Until I have stronger proof to the contrary than your looking into a pair of beautiful eyes. Have you never observed, my friend, how many pairs of beautiful eyes there are in the world?"

He shook his head. "I haven't bothered much about them, except now and then for a bit of nonsense making."

"But this pair you, too, are going to go on trusting?"

"I am. If that girl was Miss Linton she had a reason for not speaking. If it wasn't"—he drew a deep breath—"well, I don't know exactly how to explain that!"

"I do," said Ellen Burns, smiling. "She thought she would never see you again, and she yielded to a girlish desire to look hard at—a real man."

It was this speech which, in spite of himself, lingered in King's mind after she was gone, for the balm there was in it—a balm she had perfectly understood and meant to put there. Well she guessed what his disablement meant to him—in spite of the hope of complete recovery—how little he seemed to himself like the man he was before.

Certainly it was nothing short of real manhood which prompted the talk he had with his mother one day not long after this. She brought him a letter, and she was scrutinizing it closely as she came toward him. He was fathoms deep in his work and did not observe her until she spoke.

"Whom can you possibly have as a correspondent in this town, my son?" she inquired, her eyes upon the postmark, which was that of a small city a hundred miles away. It was one in which lived an old school friend of whom she had never spoken, to her recollection, in King's hearing, for the reason that the family had since suffered deep disgrace in the eyes of the world, and she had been inexpressibly shocked thereby.

King looked up. He was always hoping for a word from Anne Linton, and now, suddenly, it had come, just a week after the encounter with the girl in the car—which had been going, as it happened, in the opposite direction from the city of the postmark. He recognized instantly the handwriting upon the plain, white business envelope—an interesting handwriting, clear and black, without a single feminine flourish. He took the letter in his hand and studied it.

"It is from Miss Linton," he said, "and I am very glad to hear from her. It is the first time she has written since she went away—over two months ago."

He spoke precisely as he would have spoken if it had been a letter from any friend he had. It was like him to do this, and the surer another man would have been to try to conceal his interest in the letter the surer was Jordan King to proclaim it. The very fact that this announcement was certain to rouse his mother's suspicion that the affair was of moment to him was enough to make him tell her frankly that she was quite right.

He laid the letter on the desk before him unopened, and went on with his work. Mrs. King stood still and looked at him a moment before moving quietly away, and disturbance was written upon her face. She knew her son's habit of finishing one thing before he took up another, but she understood also that he wished to be alone when he should read this letter. She left the room, but soon afterward she softly passed the open door, and she saw that the letter lay open before him and that his head was bent over it. The words before him were these:

> Dear Mr. King:
>
> I had not meant to write to you for much longer than this, but I find myself so anxious to know how you are that I am yielding to the

temptation. I may as well confess that I am just a little lonely to-night, in spite of having had a pretty good day with the little book—rather better than usual. Sometimes I almost wish I hadn't spent that fortnight with Mrs. Burns, I find myself missing her so. And yet, how can one be sorry for any happy thing that comes to one? As I look back on them now, though I am well and strong again, those days of convalescence in the hospital stand out as among the happiest in my life. The pleasant people, the flowers, the notes, all the incidents of that time, not the least among them Franz's music, stay in my memory like a series of pictures.

Do you care to tell me how you come on? If so you may write to me, care of general delivery, in this town, at any time for the next five days. I shall be so glad to hear.

Anne Linton.

King looked up as his mother approached. He folded the letter and put it into his pocket.

"Mother," he said, "I may as well tell you something. You won't approve of it, and that is why I must tell you. From the hour I first saw Miss Linton I've been unable to forget her. I know, by every sign, that she is all she seems to be. I can't let her go out of my life without an effort to keep her. I'm going to keep her, if I can."

Two hours later R.P. Burns, M.D., was summoned to the bedside of Mrs. Alexander King. He sat down beside the limp form, felt the pulse, laid his hand upon the shaking shoulder of the prostrate lady, who had gone down before her son's decision, gentle though his manner with her had been. She had argued, prayed, entreated, wept, but she had not been able to shake his purpose. Now she was reaping the consequences of her agitation.

"My son, my only boy," she moaned as Burns asked her to tell him her trouble, "after all these years of his being such a man, to change suddenly into a willful boy again! It's inconceivable; it's not possible! Doctor, you must tell him, you must argue with him. He can't marry this girl, he can't! Why, he doesn't even know the place she comes from, to say nothing of who she is—her family, her position in life. She must be a common sort of creature to follow him up so; you know she must. I can't have it; I will not have it! You must tell him so!"

Burns considered. There was a curious light in his eyes. "My dear lady," he said gently at length, "Jordan is a man; you can't control him. He is a mighty manly man, too—as his frankly telling you his intention proves. Most sons would have kept their plans to themselves, and simply have brought the mother home her new daughter some day without any warning. As for Miss Linton, I assure you she is a lady—as it seems to me you must have seen for yourself."

"She is clever; she could act the part of a lady, no doubt," moaned the one who possessed a clear title to that form of address. "But she might be anything. Why didn't she tell you something of herself? Jordan could not say that you knew the least thing about her. People with fine family records are not so mysterious. There is something wrong about her—I know it—I know it! Oh, I can't have it so; I can't! You must stop it, Doctor; you must!"

"She spent two weeks in our home," Burns said. "During that time there was no test she did not stand. Come, Mrs. King, you know that it doesn't take long to discover the flaw in any metal. She rang true at every touch. She's a girl of education, of refinement—why, Ellen came to feel plenty of real affection for her before she left us, and you know that means a good deal. As for the mystery about her, what's that? Most people talk too much about their affairs. If, as we think, she has been brought up in circumstances very different from these we find her in, it isn't strange that she doesn't want to tell us all about the change."

But his patient continued to moan, and he could give her no consolation. For a time he sat quietly beside the couch where lay the long and slender form, and he was thinking things over. The room was veiled in a half twilight, partly the effect of closing day and partly that of drawn shades. The deep and sobbing breaths continued until suddenly Burns's hand was laid firmly upon the hand which clutched a handkerchief wet with many tears. He spoke now in a new tone, one she had never before heard from him addressed to herself:

"This," he said, "isn't worthy of you, my friend."

It was as if her breath were temporarily suspended while she listened. People were not accustomed to tell Mrs. Alexander King that her course of action was unworthy of her.

"No man or woman has a right to dictate to another what he shall do, provided the thing contemplated is not an offense against another. You have no right to set your will against your son's when it is a matter of his life's happiness."

She seized on this last phrase. "But that's why I do oppose him. I want him to be happy—heaven knows I do! He can't be happy—this way."

"How do you know that? You don't know it. You are just as likely to make him bitterly unhappy by opposing him as by letting him alone. And I can tell you one thing surely, Mrs. King: Jordan will do as he wishes in spite of you, and all you will gain by opposition will be not a gain, but a sacrifice—of his love."

She shivered. "How can you think he will be so selfish?"

Burns had some ado to keep his rising temper down. "Selfish—to marry the woman he wants instead of the woman you want? That's an old, old argument of selfish mothers."

The figure on the couch stiffened. "Doctor Burns! How can you speak so, when all I ask for is my son's best good?" The words ended in a wail.

"You think you do, dear lady. What you really want is—your own way."

Suddenly she sat up, staring at him. His clear gaze met her clouded one, his sane glance confronted her wild one. She lifted her shaking hand with a gesture of dismissal. But there was a new experience in store for Jordan King's mother.

Burns leaned forward, and took the delicate hand of his hysterical patient in his own.

"No, no," he said, smiling, "you don't mean that; you are not quite yourself. I am Jordan's friend and yours. I have said harsh things to you; it was the only way. I love your boy as I would a younger brother, and I want you to keep him because I can understand what the loss of him would mean to you. But you must know that you can't tie a man's heart to you with angry commands, nor with tears and reproaches. You can tie it—tight—by showing sympathy and understanding in this crisis of his life. Believe me, I know."

His tone was very winning; his manner—now that he had said his say—though firm, was gentle, and he held her hand in a way that did much toward quieting her. Many patients in danger of losing self-control had known the strengthening, soothing touch of that strong hand. Red Pepper was not accustomed to misuse this power of his, which came very near being hypnotic, but neither did he hesitate to use it when the occasion called as loudly as did this one.

And presently Mrs. King was lying quietly on her couch again, her eyes closed, the beating of her agitated pulses slowly quieting. And Burns, bending close, was saying before he left her: "That's a brave woman. Ladies are lovely things, but I respect women more. Only a mighty fine one could be the mother of my friend Jord, and I knew she would meet this issue like the Spartan she knows how to be."

If, as he stole away downstairs—leaving his patient in the hands of a somewhat long-suffering maid—he was saying to himself things of a quite different sort, let him not be blamed for insincerity. He had at the last used the one stimulant against which most of us are powerless: the call to be that which we believe another thinks us.

CHAPTER X

The Surgical Firing Line

"Len, I've something great to tell you," announced Red Pepper Burns, one evening in August, as he came out from his office where he had been seeing a late patient, and joined his wife, who was wandering about her garden in the twilight. "To-day I've had the compliment of my life. Whom do you think I'm to operate on day after to-morrow?"

She looked up at him as he stood, his hands in his pockets, looking down at her. In her sheer white frock, through which gleamed her neck and arms, her hands full of pink and white snapdragon, she was worth consideration. Her eyes searched his face and found there a curious exultation of a very human sort. "How could I guess? Tell me."

"Who should you say was the very last man on earth to do me the honour of trusting me in a serious emergency?"

She turned away her head, gazing down at a fragrant border of mignonette, while he watched her, a smile on his lips. She looked up again. "I can't think, Red. It seems to me everybody trusts you."

"Not by a long shot, or the rest of the profession would stand idle. But there's one man who I should have said, to use a time-honoured phrase, wouldn't let me operate on a sick cat. And he's the man who is going to put his life in my hands Wednesday morning at ten o'clock. Len, if I am ever on my mettle to do a perfect job, it'll be then!"

"Of course. But who—"

"I should think the name would leap to your lips. Who's mine ancient enemy, the man who has fought me by politely sneering at me, and circumventing me when he could, ever since I began practice, and whom I've fought back in my way? Why, Len—"

Her dark eyes grew wide. "Red! Not—Doctor Van Horn?"

"Even so."

"Oh, Red! That is a compliment—and

more than a compliment. But I should never have thought of him somehow because, I suppose—"

"Because nobody ever thinks of a doctor's being sick or needing an operation. But doctors do—sometimes—and usually pretty badly, too, before they will submit to it. Van Horn's in dreadful shape, and has been keeping it dark—until it's got the upper hand of him completely. Mighty plucky the way he's been going on with his work, with trouble gnawing at his vitals."

"How did he come to call you?"

"That's what I'm wondering. But call me he did, yesterday, and I've seen him twice since. And when I told him what had to be done he took it like a soldier without wincing. But when he said he wanted me to do the trick you could have knocked me down with a lead pencil. My word, Len, I have been doing Van an injustice all these years! The real stuff is in him, after all, and plenty of it, too."

"It is he who has done you the injustice," Ellen said with a little lift of the head.

"I know I have given you reason to think so—the times I've come home raving mad at some cut of his. But, Len, that's all past and he wipes it out by trusting me now. The biggest thing I've had against him was not his knifing me but his apparent toadying to the rich and influential. But there's another side to that and I see it now. Some people have to be coddled, and though it goes against my grain to do it, I don't know why a man who can be diplomatic and winning, like Van Horn, hasn't his place just as much as a rough rider like me. Anyhow, the thing now is to pull him through his operation, and if I can do it—well, Van and I will be on a new basis, and a mighty comfortable one it will be."

His voice was eager and his wife understood just how his pulses were thrilling, as do those of the born surgeon, at the approach of a great opportunity.

"I'm very, very glad, dear," Ellen said warmly. "It's a real triumph of faith over jealousy, and I don't wonder you are proud of such a commission. I know you will bring him through."

"If I don't—but that's not to be thought of. It's a case that calls for extremely delicate surgery and a sure hand, but the ground is plainly mapped out and only some absolutely unforeseen complication is to be dreaded. And when it comes to those complications—well, Len, sometimes I think it must be the good Lord who works a man's brain for him at such crises, and makes it pretty nearly superhuman. It's hard to account any other way, sometimes, for the success of the quick decisions you make under necessity that would take a lot of time to work out if you had the time. Oh, it's a great game, Len, no doubt of that—when you win. And when you lose"—he stopped short, staring into the shadows where a row of dark-leaved laurel bushes shut away the garden in a soft seclusion—"well, that's another story, a heartbreaking story."

He was silent for a minute, then, in another tone, he spoke confidently: "But—this isn't going to be a story of that kind. Van Horn has a big place in the city and he's going to keep it. And I'm going to spend the rest of this evening making a bit of a tool I've had in mind for some time—that there's a remote chance I shall need in this case. But if that remote chance should come—well, there's nothing like a state of preparedness, as the military men say."

"That's why you succeed, Red; you always are prepared."

"Not always. And it's in the emergency you can't foresee that heaven comes to the rescue. You can't expect it to come to the rescue when you might have foreseen. 'Trust the Lord and keep your powder dry' is a pretty good maxim for the surgical firing line, too—eh?"

With his arm through his wife's he paced several times up and down the flowery borders, then went away into the small laboratory and machine shop where he was accustomed to do much of the work which showed only in its final results. Through the rest of the hot August evening, his attire stripped to the lowest terms compatible with possible unexpected visitors, he laboured with all the enthusiasm characteristic of him at tasks which to another mind would have been drudgery indeed.

To him, at about ten o'clock, came his neighbour and friend, Arthur Chester. Standing with arms on the sill outside of the lighted window, clad in summer vestments of white and looking as cool and fresh as the man inside looked hot and dirty, Chester attempted to lure the worker forth.

"Win's serving a lot of cold, wet stuff on our porch," he announced. "Ellen's there, and the Macauleys, and Jord King has just driven up and stopped for a minute. He's got Aleck with him and he's pleased as Punch because he's rigged a contrivance so that Aleck can drive himself with one hand. What do you think of that?"

"Good work," replied Burns absently after a minute, during which he tested a steel edge with an experimental finger and shook his head at it.

"Did you expect Jord to keep Aleck, when he's got to have another man besides for the things Aleck can't do now?"

Burns nodded. "Expect anything—of him."

"Put down that murderous-looking thing and come along over. Ellen said you were here, and Win sent word to you not to bother to change your clothes."

"Thanks—I won't."

"Won't bother—or won't come?"

"Both."

Chester sighed. "Do you know what you remind me of when you get in this hole of a workshop? A bull pup with his teeth in something, and only growls issuing."

"Better keep away then."

"I suppose that's a hint—a bull-pup hint."

Silence from inside, while the worker stirred something boiling over a flame, poured a dark fluid from one retort into another, dropped in a drop or two of something from a small vial inflammatorily labelled, and started an electric motor in a corner. Chester could see the shine of perspiration on the smooth brow below the coppery hair, and drops standing like dew on the broad white chest from which the open shirt was turned widely back.

"It must be about a hundred and fifty Fahrenheit in there," he commented. Burns grunted an assent. "It's only eighty-four on our porch, and growing cooler every minute. The things we have to drink are just above thirty-two, right off the ice." Chester's words were carefully chosen.

"Dangerous extremes. But I wouldn't mind having a pint or two of something cold. Go, bring it to me."

"Well, I like that."

"So'll I, I hope."

Chester laughed and strolled away. When he returned he carried a big crystal pitcher filled with a pleasantly frothing home-made amber brew in which ice tinkled. With him came Jordan King. Chester shoved aside the screen and pushed the pitcher inside, accompanied by a glass which Winifred had insisted on sending.

Burns caught up the pitcher, drank thirstily, drew his arm across his mouth and grinned through the window, meeting Jordan King's smiling gaze in return.

"Company manners don't go when your hands are black, eh?" remarked the man inside.

"Mechanics and surgeons seem a good deal alike at times," was the laughing reply.

"Can't tell 'em apart. Your lily-handed surgeon is an anomaly. I hear Aleck came out under his own steam to-night. How does it go?"

"First rate. It was great fun. He's like a boiling kettle full of steam, with the lid off just in time."

"Good. Be on your guard when he's driving, though, for a while. Don't let him stay at the wheel down Devil's Hill just yet."

"Why not? He has absolute control the way I've fixed it. You see the spark and gas are right where—"

"I don't want you to take one chance in a million on that back of yours yet. See? Or do I have to drive that order in and spike it down?"

"He seems to have a lot of conversation in him—for you," observed Chester to King as the two outside laughed at this explosion from within.

"Such as it is," replied King with an audacious wink. "I thought I'd got about through taking orders."

"I'll give you both two minutes to clear out," came from inside the window as Burns caught up a piece of steel and began narrowly to examine it. Over it he looked at Jordan King, and the two exchanged a glance which spoke of complete understanding.

"Come again, boy," Burns said with a sudden flashing smile at his friend.

"I will—day after to-morrow in the afternoon," King returned, and his eyes held Burns's.

"What? Do you know?"

King nodded, with a look of pride. "You bet I do."

"Who told you?"

"Himself."

"Didn't know you knew him well enough for that."

"Oh, yes, through mother; they're old friends. She sent me to see him for her."

"I see. Well, wish me luck!"

"I wish you—your own skill at its highest power," said Jordan King fervently.

"Thanks, youngster," was Burns's answer, and this time there was no smile on the face which he lifted again for an instant from above the tiny piece of steel which held in it such potentialities—in his hands.

"You seem to have got farther in under his skin than the rest of us," observed Chester to King as they walked slowly away. There was a touch of unconscious jealousy in his tone. He had known R.P. Burns a long while before Jordan King had reached man's estate. "I never knew him to say a word about a coming operation before."

"He didn't say it now; I happened to know. Come out and see the rigging we've put on the car so Aleck can work everything with one hand and two feet."

"And a few brains, I should say," Chester supplemented.

Though Burns had plenty of other work to keep him busy during the interval before he should lay hands upon Doctor Van Horn, his mind was seldom off his coming task. In spite of all that Ellen knew of the past antagonism between the two men she was in possession of but comparatively few of the facts. Except where his fiery temper had entirely overcome him Burns had been silent concerning the many causes he had had to dislike and distrust the older man.

As what is called "a fashionable physician," having for his patients few outside of the wealthy class, Dr. James Van Horn had occupied a field of practice entirely different from that of R.P. Burns. Though Burns numbered on his list many of the city's best known and most prosperous citizens, he held them by virtue of a manner of address and a system of treatment differing in no wise from that which he employed upon the poorest and humblest who came to him. If people liked him it was for no blandishments of his, only for his sturdy manliness, his absolute honesty, and a certain not unattractive bluntness of speech whose humour often atoned for its thrust.

As for his skill, there was no question that it ranked higher than that of his special rival. As for his success, it had steadily increased. And, as all who knew him could testify, when it came to that "last ditch" in which lay a human being fighting for his life, Burns's reputation for standing by, sleeves rolled up and body stiff with resistance of the threatening evil, was such that there was no man to compete with him.

It was inevitable that in a city of the

moderate size of that in which these two men practised there should arise situations which sometimes brought about a clash between them. The patient of one, having arrived at serious straits, often called for a consultation with the other. The very professional bearing and methods of the two were so different, strive though they might to adapt themselves to each other at least in the presence of the patient, that trouble usually began at once, veiled though it might be under the stringencies of professional etiquette. Later, when it came to matters of life and death, these men were sure to disagree radically. Van Horn, dignified of presence, polished of speech, was apt to impress the patient's family with his wisdom, his restraint, his modestly assured sense of the fitness of his own methods to the needs of the case; while Burns, burning with indignation over some breach of faith occasioned by his senior's orders in his absence, or other indignity, flaming still more hotly over being forced into a course which he believed to be against the patient's interest, was likely to blurt out some rough speech at a moment when silence, as far as his own interests were concerned, would have been more discreet—and then would come rupture.

Usually those most concerned never guessed at the hidden fires, because even Burns, under bonds to his wife to restrain himself at moments of danger, was nearly always able to get away from such scenes without open outbreak. But more than once a situation had developed which could be handled only by the withdrawal of one or the other physician from the case—and then, whether he went or stayed, Burns could seldom win through without showing what he felt.

Now, however, he was feeling as he had never dreamed he could feel toward James Van Horn. The way in which the man was facing the present crisis in his life called for Burns's honest and ungrudging admiration. With that same cool and unflurried bearing with which Van Horn was accustomed to hold his own in a consultation was he now awaiting the uncertain issue of his determination to end, in one way or the other, the disability under which he was suffering.

CHAPTER XI

The Only Safe Place

When Red Pepper Burns visited James Van Horn, at the hospital, on the evening before the operation, he found him lying quietly in bed, ready for the night—and the morning. He looked up and smiled the same slightly frosty smile Burns knew so well, but which he now interpreted differently. As he sat down by the bedside the younger man's heart was unbelievably warm.

He looked straight, with his powerful hazel eyes slightly veiled by a contraction of the eyelids, into the steady gray eyes of his patient—his patient—he could not believe it yet. He laid exploring fingers upon the pulse of the hand he had just grasped.

"If they were all like you," he said gently, "we should have better chances for doing our best. How do you manage it, Doctor?"

"Temperament, I suppose," returned the other lightly. "Or"—and now he spoke less lightly—"belief—or lack of it. If we get through—very well; I shall go on with my work. If we don't get through—that ends it. I have no belief in any hereafter, as you may know. A few years more or less—what does it matter?"

Burns studied the finely chiselled face in silence for a minute, then he spoke slowly: "It matters this much—to me. If by a chance, a slip, a lack of skill, I should put an end to a life which would never live again, I could not bear it."

Van Horn smiled—and somehow the smile was not frosty at all. "I am trusting you. Your hand won't slip; there will be no lack of skill. If you don't pull me through, it will be because destiny is too much for us. To be honest, I don't care how it comes out. And yet, that's not quite true either. I do care; only I want to be entirely well again. I can't go on as I have gone."

"You shall not. We're going to win; I'm confident of it. Only—Doctor, if the unforeseen should happen I don't want you to go out of this life believing there's no other. Listen." He pulled out a notebook and searching, found a small newspaper clipping. "A big New York paper the other day printed this headline: '*Fell Eight Stories to Death.*' A smaller city paper copied it with this ironical comment: '*Headlines cannot be too complete. But what a great story it would have been if he had fallen eight stories to life!*' And then one of the biggest and most influential and respected newspapers in the world copied both headlines and comment and gave the whole thing a fresh title: '*Falls to Life—Immortal.*' Doctor—you can't afford to lie to-night where you do—and take chances on that last thing's not being true. The greatest minds the world knows believe it is true."

A silence fell. Then Van Horn spoke: "Burns, do you think it's wise to turn a patient's thoughts into this channel on the eve of a crisis?"

Burns regarded him closely. "Can you tell me, Doctor," he asked, "that your thoughts weren't already in that channel?"

"Suppose they were. And suppose I even admitted the possibility that you were right—which, mind you, I don't—what use is it to argue the question at this late hour?"

"Because the hour is not too late. If you want to sleep quietly to-night and wake fit for what's coming, put yourself in the hands of the Maker of heaven and earth before you sleep. Then, whether there's a hereafter or not won't matter for you; you'll leave that to Him. But you'll be in His hands—and that's the only place it's safe to be."

"Suppose I told you I didn't believe in any such Being."

"I should tell you you knew better—and knew it with every fibre of you."

The two pairs of eyes steadily regarded each other. In Burns's flamed sincerity and conviction. In Van Horn's grew a curious sort of suffering. He moved restlessly on his pillow.

"If I had known you were a fanatic as well as a fighter I might have hesitated to call you, even though I believe in you as a surgeon," he said somewhat huskily.

"It's surgery you're getting from me to-night, but I cut to cure. A mind at rest will help you through to-morrow."

"Why should you think my mind isn't at rest? You commended me for my quiet mind when you came in."

"For your cool control. But your unhappy spirit looked out of your eyes at me, and I've spoken to that. I couldn't keep silence. Forgive me, Doctor; I'm a blunt fellow, as you have reason to know. I haven't liked you, and you haven't liked me. We've fought each other all along the line. But your calling me now has touched me very much, and I find myself caring tremendously to give you the best I have. And not only the best my hands have to give you, but the best of my brain and heart. And that belief in the Almighty and His power to rule this world and other worlds is the best I have. I'd like to give it to you."

He rose, his big figure towering like a mountain of strength above the slender form in the bed.

Van Horn stretched up his hand to say good-night. "I know you thought it right to say this to me, Burns," he said, "and I have reason to know that when you think a thing is right you don't hesitate to do it. I like your frankness—better than I seem to. I trust you none the less for this talk; perhaps more. Do your best by me in the morning, and whatever happens, your conscience will be free."

Burns's two sinewy hands clasped the thin but still firm one of Van Horn. "As I said just now, I've never wanted more to do my best than for you," came very gently from his lips. "And I can tell you for your comfort that the more anxious I am to do good work the surer I am to do it. I don't know why it should be so; I've heard plenty of men say it worked just the other way with them. Yes, I do know why. I think I'll tell you the explanation. The more anxious I am the harder I pray to my God to make me fit. And when I go from my knees to the operating-room I feel armed to the teeth."

He smiled, a brilliant, heart-warming smile, and suddenly he looked, to the man on the bed who gazed at him, more like a conqueror than any one he had ever seen. And all at once James Van Horn understood why, with all his faults of temper and speech, his patients loved and clung to Red Pepper Burns; and why he, Van Horn himself, had not been able to defeat Burns as a rival. There was something about the man which spoke of power, and at this moment it seemed clear, even to the skeptic, that it was not wholly human power.

Burns bent over the bed. “Good-night, Doctor,” he said softly, almost as he might have spoken to a child. Then, quite as he might have spoken to a child, he added: “Say a bit of a prayer before you go to sleep. It won't hurt you, and—who knows?—even unbelieving, you may get an answer.”

Van Horn smiled up at him wanly. “Good-night, Doctor,” he replied. “Thank you for coming in—whether I sleep the better or the worse for it.”

If there were anything of the fanatic about Redfield Pepper Burns—and the term was one which no human being but Van Horn had ever applied to him—it was the fighting, not the fasting, side of his character which showed uppermost at ten next morning. He came out of his hospital dressing-room with that look of dogged determination written upon brow and mouth which his associates knew well, and they had never seen it written larger. From Doctor Buller, who usually gave the anesthetics in Burns's cases, and from Miss Mathewson, who almost invariably worked upon the opposite side of the operating table, to the newest nurse whose only mission was to be at hand for observation, the staff more or less acutely sensed the situation. Not one of those who had been for any length of time in the service but understood that it was an unusual situation.

That James Van Horn and R.P. Burns had long been conscious or unconscious rivals was known to everybody. Van Horn was not popular with the hospital staff, while Burns might have ordered them all to almost any deed of valour and have been loyally obeyed. But Van Horn's standing in the city was well understood; he was admired and respected as the most imposing and influential figure in the medical profession there represented. He held many posts of distinction, not only in the city, but in the state, and his name at the head of an article in any professional magazine carried weight and authority. And that he should have chosen Burns, rather than have sent abroad for any more famous surgeon, was to be considered an extraordinary honour indicative of a confidence not to have been expected.

Altogether, there was more than ordinary tension observable in the operating-room just before the appointed hour. A number of the city's surgeons were present—Grayson, Fields, Lenhart, Stevenson—men accustomed to see Burns at work and to recognize his ability as uncommon. Not that they often admitted this to themselves or to one another, but the fact remains that they understood precisely why Van Horn, if he chose a local man at all—which of itself had surprised them very much—had selected Burns. Not one of them, no matter how personally he felt antagonistic to this most constantly employed member of the profession, but would have felt safer in his hands in such a crisis than in those of any of his associates.

Burns held a brief conference with Miss Mathewson, who having been with him in his office and his operative work for the entire twelve years of his practice, was herself all but a surgeon and suited him better than any man, with her deft fingers and sure response to his slightest indication of intention. The others found themselves watching the two as they came forward, cool, steady, ready for the perfect team work they had so long played. If both hearts were beating a degree faster than usual there was nothing to show it. Nobody knew what had passed between the two. If they had known they might have understood why they worked so perfectly together.

"You're going to give me your best to-day, Amy, eh?"

"You know that, Doctor Burns."

"Of course I know it. But I want a little better than your best. This is one of the cases where every second is going to count. We have to make all the speed that's in us without a slip. I can trust you. I didn't tell you before because I didn't want you thinking about it. But I tell you now because I've got to have the speed. All right; that's all."

He gave her one quick smile, then his face was set and stern again, as always at this moment, for it was the moment when he caught sight of his patient, quietly asleep, being brought to him. And it was the moment when one swift echo of the prayer he had already made upon his knees leaped through his mind—to be gone again as lightning flashes through a midnight sky. After that there was to be no more prayer, only action.

The watching surgeons unconsciously held their breath as the operation began. For the patient on the table was James Van Horn, and the man who had taken Van Horn's life into his hands was not a great surgeon from New York or Boston, as was to have been anticipated, but their everyday colleague Burns. And at that moment not one of them envied him his chance.

Ellen had seldom waited more anxiously for the word her husband always sent her at such times. He fully recognized that the silent partner in crises like these suffered a very real and trying suspense, the greater that there was nothing she could do for him except to send him to his work heartened by the thought of her and of her belief in him.

It was longer than usual, on this more than ordinarily fateful morning, before Ellen received the first word from the hospital. When it came it was from an attendant and it was not reassuring:

"Doctor Burns wishes me to tell you that the patient has come through the operation, but is in a critical condition. He will not leave him at present."

This meant more hours of waiting, during which Ellen could set her mind and hand to nothing which was not purely mechanical. She was realizing to the full that it was the unknown factor of which Burns had often spoken, the unforeseen contingency, which might upset all the calculations and efforts of science and skill. Well she knew that, though her husband's reputation was an assured one, it might suffer somewhat from the loss of this prominent case. Ellen felt certain that this last consideration was one to weigh little with Burns himself compared with his personal and bitter regret over an unsuccessful effort to save a life. But it seemed to her that she cared from every point of view, and to her the time of waiting was especially hard to bear.

There was one relief in the situation—never had she had her vigils shared as Jordan King was sharing this one. As the hours went by, both by messages over the telephone and by more than one hurried drive out to see Ellen in person, did he let her know that his concern for Burns's victory was only second to her own.

"He's got to save him!" was his declaration, standing in her doorway, late in the evening, hat in hand, bright dark eyes on Ellen's. "And the way he's sticking by, I'm confident he will. That bull-dog grip of his we know so well would pull a ton of lead out of a quicksand. He won't give up while there's a breath stirring, and even if it stops he'll start it again—with his will!"

"You are a loyal friend." Ellen's smile

rewarded him for this blindly assured speech, well as she knew how shaky was the foundation on which he might be standing. "But the last message he sent was only that no ground had been lost."

"Well, that's a good deal after ten hours." He looked at his watch. "Keep a brave heart, Mrs. Burns. I'm going to the hospital now to see if I can get just a glimpse of our man before we settle down for the night. And I want to arrange with Miss Dwight—she was my nurse—to let me know any news at any hour in the night."

It was at three in the morning that King called her to say with a ring of joy in his voice: "There's a bit of a gain, Mrs. Burns. It looks brighter."

It was at eight, five hours later, that Burns himself spoke to her. His voice betrayed tension in spite of its steadiness. "We're holding hard, Len; that's about all I can say."

"Dear—are you getting any rest?"

"Don't want any; I'm all right. I'll not be home till we're out of this, you know.

Good-bye, my girl." And he was gone, back to the bedside. She knew, without being told, that he had hardly left it.

Thirty-six hours had gone by, and Ellen and Jordan King had had many messages from the hospital before the one came which eased their anxious minds: "Out of immediate danger." It was almost another thirty-six before Burns came home.

She had never seen him look more radiantly happy, though the shadows under his eyes were heavy, and there were lines of fatigue about his mouth. Although she had been watching for him he took her by surprise at last, coming upon her in the early morning just as she was descending the stairs. With both arms around her, as she stood on the bottom stair, he looked into her eyes.

"The game's worth the candle, Len," he said.

"Even though you've been burning the candle at both ends, dear? Yes, I know it is. I'm so glad—so glad!"

"We're sworn friends, Van and I. Can you

believe it? Len, he's simply the finest ever."

She smiled at him. "I'm sure you think so; it's just what you would think, my generous boy."

"I'll prove it to you by and by, when I've had a wink of sleep. A bath, breakfast, and two hours of rest—then I'll be in service again. Van's resting comfortably, practically out of danger, and—Len, his eyes remind me of a sick child's who has waked out of a delirium to find his mother by his side."

"Is that the way his eyes look when they meet yours?"

He nodded. "Of course. That's how I know."

"O Red," she said softly—"to think of the eyes that look at you like that!"

"They don't all," he answered as the two went up the stairs side by side. "But Van—well, he's been through the deep waters, and he's found—a footing on rock where he expected shifting sands. Ah, there's my boy! Give him to me quick!"

The Little-Un, surging plumply out of the nursery, tumbled into his father's arms, and submitted, shouting with glee, to the sort of huggings, kissings, and general inspection to which he was happily accustomed when Burns came home after a longer absence than usual.

Just before he went back to the hospital, refreshed by an hour's longer sleep than he had meant to take, because Ellen would not wake him sooner, Burns opened the pile of mail which had accumulated during his absence. He sat on the arm of the blue couch, tossing the letters one by one upon the table behind it, in two piles, one for his personal consideration, the other for Miss Mathewson's answering. Ellen, happily relaxing in a corner of the couch, her eyes watching the letter opening, saw her husband's eyes widen as he stooped to pick up a small blue paper which had fallen from the missive he had just slitted. As he unfolded the blue slip and glanced at it, an astonished whistle leaped to his lips.

"Well, by the powers—what's this?" he murmured. "A New York draft for a thousand dollars, inclosed in a letter which says nothing except a typewritten '*From One of the most grateful of all grateful patients*.' Len, what do you think of that? Who on earth sent it? I haven't had a rich patient who hasn't paid his bill, or who won't pay it in due form when he gets around to it. And the poor ones don't send checks of this size."

"I can't imagine," she said, studying the few words on the otherwise blank sheet, and the postmark on the typewritten envelope, which showed the letter also to have come from New York. "You haven't had a patient lately who was travelling—a hotel case, or anything of that sort?"

He shook his head. "None that didn't pay before he left—and none that seemed particularly grateful anyhow. Well, I must be off. The thousand's all right, wherever it came from, eh? And I want to get back to Van. I'd put that draft in the fire rather than go back to find the slightest slip in his case. I think, if I should, I'd lose my nerve at last."

CHAPTER XII

The Truth about Susquehanna

Jordan King, directing his car with necessary caution through the traffic of a small but crowded city, two hundred miles from home, suddenly threw out his clutch and jammed his brakes into urgent use. Beside him Aleck, flinging out a hasty arm to warn drivers pressing closely behind, gazed at his employer in wonder. There was absolutely nothing to stop them, and an autocratic crossing policeman just ahead was impatiently waving them forward.

But King, his eyes apparently following something or some one in the throng, which had just negotiated the crossing of the street at right angles to his own direction, spoke hurriedly: "Turn to the right here, Aleck, and wait for me at the first spot down that street where they'll let you stop."

He was out of the car and off at a dangerous slant through the procession of moving vehicles, dodging past great trucks and slipping by the noses of touring cars and coupés with apparent recklessness of consequences.

Aleck, sliding into the driver's seat and forced to lose sight of King's tall figure because of the urgency of the crowding mass behind, was moved to curious speculation. As he turned the designated corner, he was saying to himself with a chuckle: "He always was quick on the trigger, but I'll be darned if that wasn't about the hastiest move I ever saw him make. What's he after, anyhow, in this town where he just told me he didn't know a soul? Well, it's some wait for me, I'll bet."

If he could have seen his master as that young man plunged along through the crowd Aleck would have found plenty to interest him. King was doing his best to pursue and catch up with a figure which he now and again lost sight of in the throng, so that he slowed his pace lest he go by it unawares. The fear that he might thus miss and lose it sharpened his gaze and gave to his face an intent look, so that many people stared at him as he passed them, wondering what the comely, dark-eyed young man was after that he was rushing at such a pace.

There came a moment when King paused, uncertain, his heart standing still with the certainty that he was off the track and that his quarry had unconsciously doubled and eluded him. An instant later he drew a quick breath of relief, his gaze following a slender black figure as it mounted the steps of an old church which stood, dingy but still dignified, close by the highway, its open doors indicating that it had remained in this downtown district for a purpose. King sprang up the steps, then paused in the great doorway, beyond which the darkness and quiet of an empty interior silently invited passers-by to rest and reflect. At that moment a deep organ note sounded far away upon the stillness, and King took a step inside, looking cautiously about him. The figure he pursued had vanished, and after a moment more he crossed the vestibule and stood, hat in hand, gazing into the dim depths beyond.

For a little, coming as he had from the strong light of the September afternoon, he could see absolutely nothing; but as his vision cleared he was able to make out a small group of people far toward the front of the spacious interior, and the form of the organist himself before his manuals low at the right of the choir. But he had to look for some time before he could descry at the farthermost side of the church a solitary head bent upon the rail before it. Toward this point the young man slowly made his way, his heart hammering a most unwonted tattoo within his broad breast.

Several pews behind and to one side of the kneeling figure he took his place, his gaze fastened upon it. He looked his fill, secure in his own position, which was in the shadow of a great stone pillar, where the dim light from the sombre-toned windows did not touch him. And, as he looked, the conviction he had had since his first meeting with this girl deepened and strengthened into resolution. He would not lose her again, no matter what it might cost to hold her. He would not believe a man could be mistaken in that face, in that exquisite and arresting personality. There was not such another in the whole wide world.

Suddenly she turned, and evidently she saw that some one was near her, though he knew it was not possible that she had recognized him. She sat quite still for another five minutes, then rose very quietly, gathering up the remembered black handbag, and moved like a young nun into the aisle, head downbent. King slipped out of his pew, made a quick circuit around the pillar, and met her squarely as she came toward him.

He stood still in her path, and she, looking partially up to pass him with that complete ignoring of his presence which young women of breeding employ when strangers threaten to take notice, heard his low voice: "Please don't run away—from your friend!"

"Oh—Mr. King!" Her eyes, startled, met his indeed, and into her face, as she spoke his name, poured a flood of beautiful colour, at sight of which King all but lost his head.

He managed, however, to retain sufficient sanity to grasp her hand after the fashion approved as the proper sign of cordiality in meeting a valued acquaintance, and to say, in an outwardly restrained manner: "Won't you sit down again here? We can talk so much better than outside—and I must talk with you. You have no idea how hard I have tried to find you."

She seemed to hesitate for an instant, but ended by slipping into the pew by the pillar where King had been sitting, and to which he pointed her, as the most sheltered spot at hand, where the group of people at the front of the church were hidden from view, and only the now low and throbbing notes of the organ could remind the pair that they were not absolutely alone.

"This is wonderful—for me," King began, in the hushed tone befitting such a place—and the tone which suited his feelings as well. "I have thought of you a million times in these months and longed to know just how you were looking. Now that I see for myself my mind is a bit easier—and yet—I'm somehow more anxious about you than ever."

"There's no reason why you should be

anxious about me, Mr. King," she answered, her eyes releasing themselves from his in spite of his effort to hold them. "I'm doing very well, and—quite enjoying my work. How about yourself? I hardly need to ask."

"Oh, I'm coming on finely, thank you. I've plunged into my work with all the zest I ever had. Only one thing has bothered me: I seemed unable to get out of the habit of watching the mails. And they have been mighty disappointing."

"You surely couldn't expect," she said, smiling a little, "that once you were well again you should be pampered with frequent letters."

"I certainly haven't been pampered. One letter in all this time—"

"Book agents haven't much time for writing letters. And surely engineers must be busy people."

He was silent for a minute, studying her. She seemed, in spite of her youth and beauty, wonderfully self-reliant. Again, as in the room at the hospital, her quiet poise of manner struck him. And though she was once more dressed in the plainest and least costly of attire—as well as he could judge—he knew that he should be entirely willing to take her anywhere where he was known, with no mental apologies for her appearance. This thought immediately put another into his mind, on which he lost no time in acting.

"This is a great piece of luck," said he, and went on hurriedly, trying to use diplomacy, which always came hard with him: "I don't want it to slip away too soon. Why couldn't we spend the rest of the day together? I'm just on my way back home from a piece of work I've been superintending outside this city. I've plenty of time ahead of me, and I'm sure the book business can't be so pressing that you couldn't take a few hours off. If you'll venture to trust yourself to me we'll go off into the country somewhere, and have dinner at some pleasant place. Then we can talk things over—all sorts of things," he added quickly, lest this seem too pointed. "Won't you—please?"

She considered an instant, then said

frankly: "Of course that would be delightful, and I can't think of a real reason why I shouldn't do it. What time is it, please?"

"Only three o'clock. We'll have time for a splendid drive and I'll promise to get you back at any hour you say—after dinner."

"It must be early."

"It shall be. Well, then—will you wait in the vestibule out here two minutes, please? I'll have the car at the door."

Thus it happened that Aleck, four blocks away, having just comfortably settled to the reading of a popular magazine on mechanics, found himself summarily ejected from his seat, and sent off upon his own resources for a number of hours.

"Take care of yourself, Al, and have a good time out of it if you can," urged his master, and Aleck observed that King's eyes were very bright and his manner indicative of some fresh mental stimulus received during the brief time of his absence. "Have the best sort of a dinner wherever you like."

"All right, Mr. King," Aleck responded. "I hope you're going to have a good time yourself," he added, "after all the work you've done to-day. I was some anxious for fear you'd do too much."

"No chance, Aleck, with Doctor Burns's orders what they are. And I didn't do a thing but stand around and talk with the men. I'm feeling fit as a fiddle now." And King drove off in haste.

Back at the church he watched with intense satisfaction Miss Anne Linton's descent of the dusty steps. The September sunshine was hazily bright, the air was warmly caressing, and there were several hours ahead containing such an opportunity as he had not yet had to try at finding out the things he had wanted to know. Not this girl's circumstances—though he should be interested in that topic—not any affairs of hers which she should not choose to tell him; but the future relationship between herself and him—this was what he must establish upon some sort of a definite basis, if it were possible.

Out through the crowded streets into

the suburbs, on beyond these to the open country, the car took its way with as much haste as was compatible with necessary caution. Once on the open road, however, and well away, King paid small attention to covering distance. Indeed, when they had reached a certain wooded district, picturesque after the fashion of the semi-mountainous country of that part of the state, he let his car idle after a fashion most unaccustomed with him, who was usually principally concerned with getting from one place to another with the least possible waste of time.

And now he and Anne Linton were talking as they never had had the chance to talk before, and they were exploring each other's minds with the zest of those who have many tastes in common. King was confirming that of which he had been convinced by her letters, that she was thoroughly educated, and that she had read and thought along lines which had intensely interested him ever since he had reached the thinking age. To his delight he found that she could hold her own in an argument with as close reasoning, as logical deduction, as keen interpretation, as any young man he knew. And with it all she showed a certain quality of appreciation of his own side of the question which especially pleased him, because it proved that she possessed that most desirable power, rare among those of her sex as he knew them—the ability to hold herself free from undue bias.

Yet she proved herself a very girl none the less by suddenly crying out at sight of certain tall masses of shell-pink flowers growing by the roadside in a shady nook, and by insisting on getting out to pick them for herself.

"It's so much more fun," she asserted, "to choose one's own than to watch a man picking all the poorest blossoms and leaving the very best."

"Is that what we do?" King asked, his eyes feasting upon the sight of her as she filled her arms with the gay masses, her face eager with her pleasure in them.

"Yes, indeed. Or else you get out a jackknife and hack off great handfuls of them at once, and bring them back all bleeding from your ruthless attack."

"I see. And you gather them delicately, so they don't mind, I suppose. Yet—I was given to understand that 'Susquehanna' died first. I've always wondered what you did to her. I'd banked on her as the huskiest of the lot."

She flashed a quick look at him, compounded of surprise, mirth, and something else whose nature he could not guess. "'Susquehanna' was certainly a wonderful rose," she admitted.

"Yet only next morning she was sadly drooping. I know, because I received a report of her. And I lost my wager."

"You should have known better," she said demurely, her head bent over her armful of flowers, "than to make a wager on the life of a rose sent to a girl who was just coming back to life herself."

"You weren't so gentle with 'Susquehanna,' then, I take it, as you are with those wild things you have there."

"I was not gentle with her at all." Anne lifted her head with a mischievously merry look. "If you must know—I kissed her—hard!"

"Ah!" Jordan King sat back, laughing, with suddenly rising colour. "I thought as much. But I suppose I'm to take it that you did it solely because she was 'Susquehanna'—not because—"

"Certainly because she was her lovely self, cool and sweet and a glorious colour, and she reminded me—of other roses I had known. Flowers to a convalescent are only just a little less reviving than food. 'Susquehanna' cheered me on toward victory."

"Then she died happy, I'm sure."

He would have enjoyed keeping it up with nonsense of this pleasurable sort, but as soon as Anne was back in the car she somehow turned him aside upon quite different ground, just how he could not tell. He found himself led on to talk about his work, and he could not discover in her questioning a trace of anything but genuine interest. No man, however modest about himself, finds it altogether distressing to have to tell a charming girl some of his more exciting experiences. In the days of his early apprenticeship King had spent many months with a contracting engineer of reputation, who was executing a notable piece of work in a wild and even dangerous country, and the young man's memory was full of adventures connected with that period. In contrast with his present work, which was of a much more prosaic sort, it formed a chapter in his history to which it stirred him even yet to turn back, and at Anne's request he was soon launched upon it.

So the afternoon passed amidst the sights and sounds of the September country. And now and again they stopped to look at some fine view from a commanding height, or flew gayly down some inviting stretch of smooth road. By and by they were at an old inn, well up on the top of the world, which King had had in mind from the start, and to which he had taken time, an hour before, to telephone and order things he had hoped she would like. When the two sat down at a table in a quiet corner there were flowers and shining silver upon a snowy cloth, and the food which soon arrived was deliciously cooked, sustaining the reputation the place had among motorists. And in the very way in which Anne Linton filled her position opposite Jordan King was further proof that, in spite of all evidence to the contrary, she belonged to his class.

Their table was lighted with shaded candles, and in the soft glow Anne's face had become startlingly lovely. She had tucked a handful of the shell-pink wild flowers into the girdle of her black dress, and their hue was reflected in her cheeks, glowing from the afternoon's drive in the sun. As King talked and laughed, his eyes seldom off her face, he felt the enchantment of her presence grow upon him with every minute that went by.

Suddenly he blurted out a question which had been in his mind all day. "I had a curious experience a while back," he said, "when I first got out into the world. I was in Doctor Burns's car, and we met some people in a limousine, touring. They stopped to ask about the road, and there was a girl in the car who looked like you. But—she didn't recognize me by the slightest sign, so I knew of course it couldn't be you."

He looked straight at Anne as he spoke, and saw her lower her eyes for a moment with an odd little smile on her lips. She did not long evade his gaze, however, but gave him back his look unflinchingly.

"It was I," she said. "But I'm not going to tell you how I came to be there, nor why I didn't bow to you. All I want to say is that there was a reason for it all, and if I could tell you, you would understand."

Well, he could not look into her face and not trust her in whatever she might elect to do, and he said something to that effect. Whereupon she smiled and thanked him, and said she was sorry to be so mysterious. He recalled with a fresh thrill how she had looked at him at that strange meeting, for now that he knew that it was surely she, the great fact which stayed by him was that she had given him that look to remember, given it to him with intent, beyond a doubt.

They came out presently upon a long porch overhanging the shore of a small lake. The September sun was already low, and the light upon the blue hills in the distance was turning slowly to a dusky purple. The place was very quiet, for it was growing late in the tourist season, and the inn was remote from main highways of travel.

"Can't we stay here just a bit?" King asked pleadingly. "It won't take us more than an hour to get back if we go along at a fair pace. We came by a roundabout way."

With each hour that passed he was realizing more fully how he dreaded the end of this unexpected and absorbing adventure. So far none of his attempts to pave the way for other meetings, in other towns to which she might be going in the course of her book selling, had resulted in anything satisfactory. And even now Anne Linton was shaking her head.

"I think I must ask you to take me back now," she said. "I want to come into the house where I am staying not later than I usually do."

So he had to leave the pleasant, vine-clad porch and take his place beside her in the car again. It did not seem to him that he was having a fair chance. But he thought of a plan and proceeded to put it into execution. He drove steadily and in silence until the lights of the nearing city were beginning to show faintly in the twilight, with the sky still rich with colour in the west. Then, at a certain curve in the road far above the rest of the countryside, he brought the car to a standstill.

"I can't bear to go on and end this day," he said in a low voice of regret. "How can I tell when I shall see you again? Do you realize that every time I have said a word about our meeting in the future you've somehow turned me aside? Do you want me to understand that you would rather never see me again?"

Her face was toward the distant lights, and she did not answer for a minute. Then she said slowly: "I should like very much to see you again, Mr. King. But you surely understand that I couldn't make appointments with you to meet me in other towns. This has happened and it has been very pleasant, but it wouldn't do to make it keep happening. Even though I travel about with a book to sell, I—shall never lose the sense of—being under the protection of a home such as other girls have."

"I wouldn't have you lose it—good heavens, no! I only—well—" And now he stopped, set his teeth for an instant, and then plunged ahead. "But there's something I can't lose either, and it's—you!"

She looked at him then, evidently startled. "Mr. King, will you drive on, please?" she said very quietly, but he felt something in her tone which for an instant he did not understand. In the next instant he thought he did understand it.

He spoke hurriedly: "You don't know me very well yet, do you? But I thought you knew me well enough to know that I wouldn't say a thing like that unless I meant all that goes with it—and follows it. You see—I love you. If—if you are not afraid of a man in a plaster jacket—it'll come off some day, you know—I ask you to marry me."

There was a long silence then, in which King felt his heart pumping away for dear life. He had taken the bit between his teeth now, certainly, and offered this girl, of whom he knew less than of any human being in whom he had the slightest interest, all that he had to give. Yet—he was so sure he knew her that, the words once out, he realized that he was glad he had spoken them.

At last she turned toward him. "You are a very brave man," she said, "and a very chivalrous man."

He laughed rather huskily. "It doesn't take much of either bravery or chivalry for a man to offer himself to you."

"It must take plenty of both. You are—what you are, in the big world you live in. And you dare to trust an absolute stranger, whom you have no means of knowing better, with that name of yours. Think, Mr. Jordan King, what that name means to you—and to your mother."

"I have thought. And I offer it to you. And I do know what you are. You can't disguise yourself—any more than the Princess in the fairy tale. Do you think all those notes I had from you at the hospital didn't tell the story? I don't know why you are selling books from door to door—and I don't want to know. What I do understand is—that you are the first of your family to do it!"

"Mr. King," she said gravely, "women are very clever at one thing—cleverer than men. With a little study, a little training, a little education, they can make a brave showing. I have known a shopgirl who, after six months of living with a very charming society woman, could play that woman's part without mistake. And when it came to talking with men of brains, she could even use a few clever phrases and leave the rest of the conversation to them, and they were convinced of her brilliant mind."

"You have not been a shopgirl," he said steadily. "You belong in a home like mine. If you have lost it by some accident, that is only the fortune of life. But you can't disguise yourself as a commonplace person, for you're not. And—I can't let you go out of my life—I can't."

Again silence, while the sunset skies slowly faded into the dusky blue of night, and the lights over the distant city grew brighter and brighter. A light wind, warmly smoky with the pleasant fragrance of burning bonfires, touched the faces of the two in the car and blew small curly strands of hair about Anne Linton's ears.

Presently she spoke. "I am going to promise to write to you now and then," she said, "and give you each time an address where you may answer, if you will promise not to come to me. I am going to tell you frankly that I want your letters."

"You want my letters—but not me?"

"You put more of yourself into your letters than any one else I know. So in admitting that I want your letters I admit that I want yourself—as a good friend."

"No more than that?"

"That's quite enough, isn't it, for people who know each other only as we do?"

"It's not enough for me. If it's enough for you, then—well, it's as I thought."

"What did you think?"

He hesitated, then spoke boldly: "No woman really wants—a mangled human being for her own."

Impulsively she laid her hand on his. Instantly he grasped it. "Please," she said, "will you never say—or think—that, again?"

He gazed eagerly into her face, still duskily visible to his scrutiny. "I won't," he answered, "if you'll tell me you care for me. Oh, don't you?—don't you?—not one bit? Just give me a show of a chance and I'll make you care. I've *got* to make you care. Why, I've thought of nothing but you for months—dreamed of you, sleeping and waking. I can't stop; it's too late. Don't ask me to stop—Anne—dear!"

No woman in her senses could have doubted the sincerity of this young man.

That he was no adept at love making was apparent in the way he stumbled over his phrases; in the way his voice caught in his throat; in the way it grew husky toward the last of this impassioned pleading of his.

He still held her hand close. "Tell me you care—a little," he begged of her silence.

"No girl can be alone as I am now and not be touched by such words," she said very gently after a moment's hesitation. "But—promising to marry you is a different matter. I can't let you rashly offer me so much when I know what it would mean to you to bring home a—book agent to your mother!"

He uttered a low exclamation. "My life is my own, to do with as I please. If I'm satisfied, that's enough. You are what I want—all I want. As for my mother—when she knows you—But we'll not talk of that just yet. What I must know is—do you—can you—care for me—enough to marry me?" His hand tightened on hers, his voice whispered in her ear: "Anne, darling—can't you love me? I want you so—oh—I want you so! Let me kiss you—just once, dear. That will tell you—"

But she drew her hand gently but efficiently away; she spoke firmly, though very low: "No—no! Listen—Jordan King. Sometime—by next spring perhaps, I shall be in the place I call home. When that time comes I will let you know. If you still care to, you may come and see me there. Now—won't you drive on, please?"

"Yes, if you'll let me—just once—*once* to live on all those months! Anne—"

But, when he would have made action and follow close upon the heels of pleading he found himself gently but firmly prevented by an uplifted small hand which did not quite touch his nearing face. "Ah, don't spoil that chivalry of yours," said her mellow, low voice. "Let me go on thinking you are what I have believed you are all along. Be patient, and prove whether this is real, instead of snatching at what might dull your judgment!"

"It wouldn't dull it—only confirm it.

And—I want to make you remember me."

"You have provided that already," she admitted, at which he gave an ejaculation as of relief—and of longing—and possibly of recognition of her handling of the whole—from her point of view—rather difficult situation. At the back of his mind, in spite of his disappointment at being kept at arm's length when he wanted something much more definite, was the recognition that here was precisely the show of spirit and dignity which his judgment approved and admired.

"I'll let you go, if I must; but I'll come to you—if you live in a hovel—if you live in a cave—if you live—Oh, I know how you live!"

"How do I live?" she asked, laughing a little unsteadily, and as if there were tears in her eyes, though of this he could not be sure.

"You live in a plain little house, with just a few of the things you used to have about you; rows of books, a picture or two, and some old china. Things may be a bit shabby, but everything is beautifully neat, and there are garden flowers on the table, perhaps white lilacs!"

"Oh, what a romanticist!" she said, through her soft laughter. "One would think you wrote novels instead of specifications for concrete walls. What if you come and find me living with my older sister, who sews for a living, plain sewing, at a dollar a day? And we have a long credit account at the grocery, which we can't pay? And at night our little upstairs room is full of neighbours, untidy, loud-talking, commonplace women? And the lamp smokes—"

"It wouldn't smoke; you would have trimmed it," he answered, quickly and with conviction. "But, even if it were all like that, you would still be the perfect thing you are. And I would take you away—"

"If you don't drive on, Mr. King," she interposed gently, "you will soon be mentally unfit to drive at all. And I must be back before the darkness has quite fallen. And—don't you think we have talked enough about ourselves?"

"I like that word," he declared as he obediently set the car in motion. "Ourselves—that sounds good to me. As long as you keep me with you that way I'll try to be satisfied. One thing I'm sure of: I've something to work for now that I didn't have this morning. Oh, I know; you haven't given me a thing. But you're going to let me come to see you next spring, and that's worth everything to me. Meanwhile, I'll do my level best—for you."

When he drew up before the door of the church, where, in spite of his entreaties that he be allowed to take her to her lodging place, Anne insisted on being left, he felt, in spite of all he had gained that day, a sinking of the heart. Though the hour was early and the neighbourhood at this time of day a quiet one, and though she assured him that she had not far to go, he was unhappy to leave her thus unaccompanied.

"I wish I could possibly imagine why it must be this way," he said to himself as he stood hat in hand beside his car, watching Anne Linton's quickly departing figure grow more and more shadowy as the twilight enveloped it. "Well, one thing is certain: whatever she does there's a good and sufficient reason; and I trust her."

CHAPTER XIII

Red Headed Again

Crowding his hat upon his head with a vigorous jerk after his reluctant parting with Anne Linton at the church door, Jordan King jumped into his car and made his way slowly through the streets to the hotel where Aleck awaited him. For the first few miles out of the city he continued to drive at a pace so moderate that Aleck more than once glanced surreptitiously at him, wondering if he were actually going to sleep at the wheel. It was not until they were beyond the last environs and far out in the open country that, quite suddenly, the car was released from its unusual restraint and began to fly down the road toward home at the old wild speed.

Somehow or other, after this encounter, King could not settle down to his work till he had seen Red Pepper Burns. He could not have explained why this should be so, for he certainly did not intend to tell his friend of the meeting with Anne Linton, or of the basis upon which his affairs now stood. But he wanted to see Burns with a sort of hunger which would not be satisfied, and he went to look him up one evening when he himself had returned early from his latest trip to the concrete dam.

He found Burns just setting forth on a drive to see a patient in the country, and King invited himself to go with him, running his own car off at one side of the driveway and leaping into Burns's machine with only a gay by-your-leave apology. But he had not more than slid into his seat before he found that he was beside a man whom he did not know.

King had long understood that Red Pepper's significant cognomen stood for the hasty temper which accompanied the coppery hair and hazel eyes of the man with the big heart. But such exhibitions of that temper as King had witnessed had been limited to quick explosions from which the smoke had cleared away almost as soon as the sound of warfare had died upon the air. He was in no way prepared, therefore, to find himself in the company of a man who was so angry that he could not—or would not—speak to one of his best friends.

"Fine night," began the young man lightly, trying again, after two silent miles, to make way against the frost in the air. "I don't know when we've had such magnificent September weather."

No answer.

"I hope you don't mind my going along. You needn't talk at all, you know—and I'll be quiet, too, if you prefer."

No answer. King was not at all sure that Burns heard him. The car was running at a terrific pace, and the profile of the man at the wheel against the dusky landscape looked as if it were carved out of stone. The young man fell silent, wondering. Almost, he wished he had not been so sure of his welcome, but there was no retreating now.

Five miles into the country they ran, and King soon guessed that their destination might be Sunny Farm, a home for crippled children which was Ellen Burns's special charity, established by herself on a small scale a few years before and greatly grown since in its size and usefulness. Burns was its head surgeon and its devoted patron, and he was accustomed to do much operative work in its well-equipped surgery, bringing out cases which he found in the city slums or among the country poor, with total disregard for any considerations except those of need and suffering. King knew that the place and the work were dearer to the hearts of both Doctor and Mrs. Burns than all else outside their own home, and he began to understand that if anything had gone wrong with affairs there Red Pepper would be sure to take it seriously.

Quite as he had foreseen—since there were few homes on this road, which ran mostly through thickly wooded country—the car rushed on to the big farmhouse, lying low and long in the night, with pleasant lights twinkling from end to end. Burns brought up with a jerk beside the central porch, leaped out, and disappeared inside without a word of explanation to his companion, who sat wondering and looking in through the open door to the wide hall which ran straight through the house to more big porches on the farther side.

Everything was very quiet at this hour, according to the rules of the place, all but the oldest patients being in bed and asleep by eight o'clock. Therefore when, after an interval, voices became faintly audible, there was nothing to prevent their reaching the occupant of the car.

In a front room upstairs at one side of the hall two people were speaking, and presently through the open window Burns was heard to say with incisive sternness: "I'll give you exactly ten minutes to pack your bag and go—and I'll take you—to make sure you do go."

A woman's voice, in a sort of deep-toned wail, answered: "You aren't fair to me, Doctor Burns; you aren't fair! You—"

"Fair!" The word was a growl of suppressed thunder. "Don't talk of fairness—you! You don't know the meaning of the word. You haven't been fair to a single kid under this roof, or to a nurse—or to any one of us—you with your smiles—and your hypocrisy—you who can't be trusted. That's the name for you—She-Who-Can't-Be-Trusted. Go pack that bag, Mrs. Soule; I won't hear another word!"

"Oh, Doctor—"

"Go, I said!"

Outside, in the car, Jordan King understood that if the person to whom Burns was speaking had not been a woman that command of his might have been accompanied by physical violence, and the offending one more than likely have been ejected from the door by the thrust of two vigorous hands on his shoulders. There was that in Burns's tone—all that and more. His wrath was quite evidently no explosion of the moment, but the culmination of long irritation and distrust, brought to a head by some overt act which had settled the offender's case in the twinkling of an eye.

Burns came out soon after, followed by a woman well shrouded in a heavy veil.

King jumped out of the car. "I'm awfully sorry," he tried to say in Burns's ear. "Just leave me and I'll walk back."

"Ride on the running board," was the

answer, in a tone which King knew meant that he was requested not to argue about it.

Therefore when the woman—to whom he was not introduced—was seated, he took his place at her feet. To his surprise they did not move off in the direction from which they had come, but went on over the hills for five miles farther, driving in absolute silence, at high speed, and arriving at a small station as a train was heard to whistle far off somewhere in the darkness.

Burns dashed into the station, bought a ticket, and had his passenger aboard the train before it had fairly come to a standstill at the platform. King heard him say no word of farewell beyond the statement that a trunk would be forwarded in the morning. Then the whole strange event was over; the train was only a rumble in the distance, and King was in his place again beside the man he did not know.

Silence again, and darkness, with only the stars for light, and the roadside rushing past as the car flew. Then suddenly, beside the deep woods, a stop, and Burns getting out of the car, with the first voluntary words he had spoken to King that night.

"Sit here, will you? I'll be back—sometime."

"Of course. Don't hurry."

It was an hour that King sat alone, wondering. Where Burns had gone, he had no notion, and no sound came back to give him hint. As far as King knew there was no habitation back there in the depths into which his companion had plunged; he could not guess what errand took him there.

At last came a distant crashing as of one making his way through heavy undergrowth, and the noise drew nearer until at length Burns burst through into the road, wide of the place where he had gone in. Then he was at the car and speaking to King, and his voice was very nearly his own again.

"Missed my trail coming back," he said. "I've kept you a blamed long time, haven't I?"

"Not a bit. Glad to wait."

"Of course that's a nice, kind lie at this time of night, and when you've no idea what you've been waiting for. Well, I'll tell you, and then maybe you'll be glad you assisted at the job."

He got in and drove off, not now at a furious pace, but at an ordinary rate of speed which made speech possible. And after a little he spoke again. "Jord," he said, "you don't know it, but I can be a fiend incarnate."

"I don't believe it," refused King stoutly.

"It's absolutely true. When I get into a red rage I could twist a neck more easily than I can get a grip on myself. Sometimes I'm afraid I'll do it. Years back when I had a rush of blood to the head of that sort I used to take it out in swearing till the atmosphere was blue; but I can't do that any more."

"Why not?" King asked, with a good deal of curiosity.

"I did it once too often—and the last time I sent a dying soul to the other world with my curses in its ears—the soul of a child, Jord. I lost my head because his mother had disobeyed my orders, and the little life was going out when it might have stayed. When I came to myself I realized what I'd done—and I made my vow. Never again, no matter what happened! And I've kept it. But sometimes, as to-night—Well, there's only one thing I can do: keep my tongue between my teeth as long as I can, and then—get away somewhere and smash things till I'm black and blue."

"That's what you've been doing back in the woods?" King ventured to ask.

"Rather. Anyhow, it's evened up my circulation and I can be decent again. I'm not going to tell you what made me rage like the bull of Bashan, for it wouldn't be safe yet to let loose on that. It's enough that I can treat a good comrade like you as I did and still have him stand by."

"I felt a good deal in the way, but I'm glad now I was with you."

"I'm glad, too, if it's only that you've discovered at last what manner of man I am when the evil one gets hold of me. None of us likes to be persistently overrated, you know."

"I don't think the less of you for being angry when you had a just cause, as I know you must have had."

"It's not the being angry; it's the losing control."

"But you didn't."

"Didn't I?" A short, grim laugh testified to Burns's opinion on this point. "Ask that woman I put on the train to-night. Jord, on her arm is a black bruise where I gripped her when she lied to me; I gripped her—a woman. You might as well know. Now—keep on respecting me if you can."

"But I do," said Jordan King.

CHAPTER XIV

A Strange Day

"Len, will you go for a day in the woods with me?"

Ellen Burns looked up from the old mahogany secretary which had been hers in the southern-home days. She was busily writing letters, but the request, from her busy husband, was so unusual that it arrested her attention. Her glance travelled from his face to the window and back again.

"I know it's pretty frosty," he acknowledged, "but the sun is bright, and I'll build you a windbreak that'll keep you snug. I'm aching for a day off—with you."

"Artful man! You know I can't resist when you put it that way, though I ought not to leave this desk for two hours. Give me half an hour, and tell me what you want for lunch."

"Cynthia and I'll take care of that. She's putting up the stuff now, subject to your approval."

He was off to the kitchen, and Ellen finished the note she had begun, put away the writing materials and letters, and ran up to her room. By the end of the stipulated half hour she was down again, trimly clad in a suit of brown tweeds, with a big coat for extra warmth and a close hat and veil for breeze resistance.

"That's my girl! You never look prettier to my eyes than when you are dressed like this. It's the real comrade look you have then, and I feel as if we were shoulder to shoulder, ready for anything that might come."

"Just as if it weren't always that," she said in merry reproach as she took her place beside him and the car rolled off.

"It's always great fun to go off with you unexpectedly like this," she went on presently. "It seems so long since we've done it. It's been such a busy year. Is everybody getting well to-day, that you can manage a whole day?"

"All but one, and he doesn't need me just now. I could keep busy, of course, but I got a sudden hankering for a day all alone with you in the woods; and after that idea once struck me I'd have made way for it anyhow, short of actually running away from duty."

"You need it, I know. We'll just leave all care behind and remember nothing except how happy we are to be together. That never grows old, does it, Red?"

"Never!" He spoke almost with solemnity, and gave her a long look as he said it, which she met with one to match it. "You dear!" he murmured. "Len, do you know I never loved you so well as I do to-day?"

"I wonder why?" She was smiling, and her colour, always duskily soft in her cheek, grew a shade warmer. "Is it the brown tweeds?"

"It's the brown tweeds, and the midnight-dark hair, and the beautiful black eyes, and—the lovely soul of my wife."

"Why, Red, dear—and all this so early in the morning? How will you end if you begin like this?"

"I don't know—or care." Something strange looked out of his eyes for a minute. "I know what I want to say now and I'm saying it. So much of the time I'm too busy to make love to my wife, I'm going to do it to-day—all day. I warn you now, so you can sidetrack me if you get tired of it."

"I'm very likely to," she said with a gay tenderness. "To have you make love to me without the chance of a telephone call to break in will be a wonderful treat."

"It sure will to me."

It was a significant beginning to a strange day. They drove for twenty miles, to find a certain place upon a bluff overlooking a small lake of unusual beauty, far out of the way of the ordinary motor traveller. They climbed a steep hill, coming out of the wooded hillside into the full sunlight of the late October day, where spread an extended view of the countryside, brilliant with autumn foliage. The air was crisp and invigorating, and a decided breeze was stirring upon this lofty point, so that the windbreak which Burns began at once to build was a necessary protection if they were to remain long.

An hour of hard work, at which Ellen helped as much as she was allowed, established a snug camp, its back against a great bowlder, its windward side sheltered by a thick barrier of hemlocks cleverly placed, a brisk bonfire burning in an angle where an improvised chimney carried off its smoke and left the corner clear and warm.

"There!" Burns exclaimed in a tone of satisfaction as he threw himself down upon the pine needle-strewn ground at Ellen's side. "How's this for a comfortable nest? Think we can spend six contented hours here, my honey?"

"Six days if you like. How I wish we could!"

"So do I. Jove, how I'd like it! I haven't had enough of you to satisfy me for many a moon. And there's no trying to get it, except by running away like this."

"We ought to do it oftener."

"We ought, but we can't. At least we couldn't. Perhaps now—"

He broke off, staring across the valley where the lake lay to the distant hills, smoky blue and purple in spite of the clear sunlight which lay upon them.

"Perhaps now—what?"

"Well—I might not be able to keep up my activity forever, and the time might come when I should have to take less work and more rest."

"But you said 'now.'"

"Did I? I was just looking ahead a bit. Len, are you hungry, or shall we wait a while for lunch?"

"Don't you want a little sleep before you eat? You haven't had too much of it lately."

"It would taste rather good—if I might take it with my head in your lap."

She arranged her own position so that she could maintain it comfortably, and he extended his big form at full length upon the rug he had brought up from the car and upon which she was already sitting. He smiled up into her face as he laid his head upon her knees, and drew one of her hands into his. "Now your little boy is perfectly content," he said.

It was an hour before he stirred, an hour in which Ellen's eyes had silently noted that which had escaped them hitherto, a curious change in his colour as he lay with closed eyes, a thinness of the flesh over the cheek bones, dark shadows beneath the eyes. Whether he slept she could not be sure. But when he sat up again these signs of wear and tear seemed to vanish at the magic of his smile, which had never been brighter. Nevertheless she watched him with a new sense of anxiety, wondering if there might really be danger of his splendid physique giving way before the rigour of his life.

She noted that he did not eat heartily at lunch, though he professed to enjoy it; and afterward he was his old boyish self for a long time. Then he grew quiet, and a silence fell between the pair while they sat looking off into the distance, the October sunlight on their heads.

And then, quite suddenly, something happened.

"Red! What is the matter?" Ellen asked, startled.

In spite of the summer warmth of the spot in which they sat her husband's big frame had begun to quiver and shake before her very eyes. Evidently he was trying hard to control the strange fit of shivering which had seized him.

"Don't be s-scared, d-dear," he managed to get out between rigid jaws. "It's just a bit of a ch-chill. I'll b-be all right in a m-minute."

"In all this sunshine? Why, Red!" Ellen caught up the big coat she had brought to the place and laid it about his shoulders—"you must have taken cold. But how could you? Come—we must go at once."

"N-not just yet. I'll g-get over this s-soon."

He drew his arms about his knees, clasping them and doing his best to master the shivering, while Ellen watched him anxiously. Never in her life with Red had she seen him cold. His rugged frame, accustomed to all weathers, hardened by years of sleeping beside wide-opened windows in the wintriest of seasons, was always healthily glowing with warmth when others were frankly freezing.

The chill was over presently, but close upon its heels followed reaction, and Red Pepper's face flushed feverishly as he said, with a gallant attempt at a smile: "Sit down again a minute, dear, while I tell you what I'm up against. I wasn't sure, but this looks like it. You've got to know now, because I'm undoubtedly in for a bit of trouble—and that means you, too."

She waited silently, but her hand slipped into his. To her surprise he drew it gently away. "Try the other one," he said. "It's in better shape for holding."

She looked down at the hand he had withdrawn and which now lay upon his knee. It was the firmly knit and sinewy hand she knew so well, the typical hand of the surgeon with its perfectly kept, finely sensitive fingertips, its broad and powerful thumb, its strong but not too thick wrist. Not a blemish marked its fair surface, yet—was it very slightly swollen? She could hardly be sure.

"Dear, tell me," she begged. "What has happened? Are you hurt—or ill—and haven't let me know?"

"I thought it might not amount to anything; it's only a scratch in the palm. But—"

"Red—did you get it—operating? On what?"

He nodded. "Operating. It's the usual way, the thing we all expect to get some day. I've been lucky so far; that's all."

"But—you didn't give yourself a scratch; you never have done that?"

"No, not up to date anyhow. I might easily enough; I just haven't happened to."

"Amy didn't?—She couldn't!"

"She didn't—and couldn't, thank heaven. She'd kill herself if she ever did that unlucky trick. No, she wasn't assisting this time. It was an emergency case, early yesterday morning—one of the other men brought in the case. It was hopeless, but the family wanted us to try."

"What sort of a case, Red?" Ellen's very lips had grown white.

"Now see here, sweetheart, I had to tell you because I knew I was in for a little trouble, but there's no need of your knowing any more than this about it. It was just an accident—nobody's fault. The blamed electric lights went off—for not over ten seconds, but it was the wrong ten seconds. I didn't even know I was scratched till the thing began to set up a row. I don't even yet understand how I got it in the palm. That's unusual."

"Who did it?"

"I'm not going to tell you. He feels badly enough now, and it wasn't his fault. He asked me at the time if he had touched me in the dark and I said no. It was as slight a thing as that. If we'd known it at the time we'd have fixed it up. We didn't, and that's all there was to it."

"You must tell me what sort of a case it was, Red."

He looked down at her. The two pairs of eyes met unflinchingly for a minute, and each saw straight into the depths of the other. Burns thought the eyes into which he gazed had never been more beautiful; stabbed though they were now with intense shock, they were yet speaking to him such utter love as it is not often in the power of man to inspire.

He managed still to talk lightly. "I expect you know. What's the use of using scientific terms? The case was rottenly septic; never mind the cause. But—I'm going to be able to throw the thing off. Just give me time."

"Let me see it, Red."

Reluctantly he turned the hand over, showing the small spot in which was quite clearly the beginning of trouble. "Doesn't look like much, does it?" he said.

"And it is not even protected."

"What was the use? The infection came

at the time."

"And you did all that work in the windbreak. Oh, you ought not to have done that!"

"Nonsense, dear. I wanted to, and I did it mostly with my left hand anyhow."

"Your blood must be of the purest," she said steadily.

"It sure is. I expect I'll get my reward now for letting some things alone that many men care for, and that I might have cared for, too—if it hadn't been for my mother—and my wife."

"You are strong—strong."

"I am—a regular Titan. Yes, we'll fight this thing through somehow; only I have to warn you it'll likely be a fight. I'll go to the hospital."

"No!" It was a cry.

"No? Better think about that. Hospital's the best place for such cases."

"It can't be better than home—when

it's like ours. We'll fight our fight there, Red—and nowhere else."

He put one hand to his arm suddenly with an involuntary movement and a contraction of the brow. But in the next breath he was smiling again. "Perhaps we'd better be getting back," he admitted. "My head's beginning to be a trifle unsteady. But, I'm glad a thousand times we've had this day."

"Was it wise to take it, dear?"

"I'm sure of it. What difference could it make? Now we've had it—to remember."

She shivered, there in the warm October sunlight. A chill seemed suddenly to have come into the air, and to have struck her heart.

No more words passed between them until they were almost home. Then Ellen said, very quietly: "Red, would you be any safer in the hospital than at home?"

"Not safer, but where it would be easier for all concerned, in case things get rather thick."

"Easier for you, too?"

He looked at her. "Do I have to speak the truth?"

"You must. If you would rather be there—"

"I would rather be as near you as I can stay. There's no use denying that. But Van Horn wants me at the hospital."

"Is he to look after you?"

"Yes. Queer, isn't it? But he wants the job. No," at the unspoken question in her face, "it wasn't Van. But he came in just as the trouble began to show and—well, you know we're the best of friends now, and I think I'd rather have him—and Buller, good old Buller—than anybody else."

"Oh, but you won't need them both?" she cried, and then bit her lip.

"Of course not. But you know how the profession are—if one of them gets down they all fall over one another to offer their services."

"They may all offer them, but they will

have to come to you. You are going to stay at home. You shall have the big guest room—made as you want it. Just tell me what to do—"

"You may as well strip it," he told her quietly. "And—Len, I'd rather be right there than anywhere else in the world. I think, when it's ready, I'll just go to bed. I'd bluff a bit longer if I could, but—perhaps—"

"I'm sure you ought," she said as quietly as he. But she was very glad when the car turned in at the driveway.

CHAPTER XV

Cleared Decks

Two hours later, under her direction and with her efficient help, Cynthia and Johnny Carruthers in medical parlance had "stripped" the guest room, putting it into the cleared bare order most useful for the purpose needed. If Ellen's heart was heavy as she saw the change made she let nothing show. And when, presently, she called her husband from the couch where he had lain, feverish and beginning to be tortured by pain, and put him between the cool, fresh sheets, she had her reward in the look he gave, first at the room and then at her.

"Decks all cleared for action," he commented with persistent cheerfulness, "and the captain on deck. Well—let them begin to fire; we're ready. All I know is that I'm glad I'm on your ship. Just pray, Len, will you—that I keep my nerve?"

This was the beginning, as Burns himself had foreseen, of that which proved indeed to be a long fight. Strong of physique though he unquestionably was, pure as was the blood which flowed in his veins, the poison he had received unwittingly and therefore taken no immediate measures to combat was able to overcome his powers of resistance and take shattering hold upon his whole organism. There followed day after day and week after week of prostrating illness, during which he suffered much torturing pain in the affected hand and arm, with profound depression of mind and body, though he bore both as bravely as was to have been expected. Two nurses, Amy Mathewson and Selina Arden, alternated in attendance upon him, day and night, and Ellen herself was always at hand to act as substitute, or to share in the care of the patient when it was more than ordinarily exacting.

As she watched the powerful form of her husband grow daily weaker before the assaults of one of the most treacherous enemies modern science has to face, she felt herself in the grip of a great dread which could not be for an hour thrown off. She did not let go of her courage; but beneath all her serenity of manner—remarked often in wonder by the nurses and physicians—lay the fear which at times amounted to a conviction that for her had come the end of earthly happiness.

She was able to appreciate none the less the devoted and skillful attention given to Burns by his colleagues. Dr. Max Buller had long been his attached friend and ally, and of him such service as he now rendered was to have been counted on. But concerning Dr. James Van Horn, although Ellen well knew how deeply he felt in Burns's debt for having in all probability saved his life only a few months earlier, she had had no notion what he had to offer in return. She had not imagined how warm a heart really lay beneath that polished urbanity of manner with its suggestion of coldness in the very tone of his voice—hitherto. She grew to feel a distinct sense of relief and dependence every time he entered the door, and his visits were so many that it came to seem as if his motor were always standing at the curb.

"You know, Len, Van's a tremendous trump," Burns himself said to her suddenly, in the middle of one trying night when Doctor Van Horn had looked in unexpectedly to see if he might ease his patient and secure him a chance of rest after many hours of pain. "It seems like a queer dream, sometimes, to open my eyes and see him sitting there, looking at me as if I were a younger brother and he cared a lot."

"He does care," Ellen answered positively. "You would be even surer of it if you could hear him talk with me alone. He speaks of you as if he loved you—and what is there strange about that? Everybody loves you, Red. I'm keeping a list of the people who come to ask about you and send you things. You haven't heard of half of them. And to-day Franz telephoned to offer to come and play for you some night when you couldn't sleep with the pain. He begged to be allowed to do the one thing he could to show his sympathy."

"Bless his heart! I'd like to hear him. I often wish my ears would stretch to reach him in his orchestra." Burns moved restlessly as he spoke. A fresh invasion of trouble in his hand and arm was reaching a culmination, and no palliative measures could ease him long.

"You've no idea, Len," he whispered as Ellen's hand strayed through his heavy coppery locks with the soothing touch he loved well, "what it means to me to have you stand by me like this. If I give in now it won't be for want of your supporting courage."

"It's you who have the courage, Red—wonderful courage."

He shook his head. "It's just the thought of you—and the Little-Un—and Bobby Burns—that's all. If it wasn't for you—"

He turned away his head. She knew the thing he had to fear—the thing she feared for him. Though his very life was in danger it was not that which made the threatening depths of black shadow into which he looked. If he should come out of this fight with a crippled right hand there would be no more work for him about which he could care. Neither Van Horn nor Buller would admit that there was danger of this; but Grayson, who had seen the hand yesterday; Fields, who was making blood counts for the case; Lenhart and Stevenson, who had come to make friendly calls every few days and who knew from Fields how things were going—all were shaking their heads and saying in worried tones that it looked pretty "owly" for the hand, and that Van Horn and Buller would do well if they pulled Burns through at all.

Outside of the profession Jordan King was closest in touch with Burns's case. He persistently refused to believe that all would not come out as they desired. He came daily, brought all sorts of offerings for the patient's comfort, and always ran up to see his friend, hold his left hand for a minute and smile at him, without a hint in his ruddy face of the wrench at the heart he experienced each time at sight of the steadily increasing devastation showing in the face on the pillow.

"You're a trump, Jord," Burns said weakly to him one morning. King had just finished a heart-warming report of certain messages brought from some of Burns's old chronic patients in the hospital wards, where it was evident the young man had gone on purpose to collect them. "Every time I look at you I think what an idiot I was ever to imagine you needed me to put backbone into you, last spring."

"But I did—and you did it. And if you think I showed more backbone to go through a thing that hardly took it out of me at all than you to stand this devilish slow torture and weakness—well, it just shows you've lost your usual excellent judgment. See?"

"I see that you're one of the best friends a man ever had. There's only one other who could do as much to keep my head above water—and he isn't here."

"Why isn't he? Who is he?" demanded King eagerly. "Tell me and I'll get him."

"No, no. He could do no more than is being done. I merely get to thinking of him and wishing I could see him. It's my old friend and chum of college days, John Leaver, of Baltimore."

"The big surgeon I've heard you and Mrs. Burns speak of? Great heavens, he'd come in a minute if he knew!"

"I've no doubt he would, but I happen to

know he's abroad just now."

King studied his friend's face, saw that Burns was already weary with the brief visit, and soon went away. But it was to a consultation with Mrs. Burns as to the possibility of communicating with Doctor Leaver.

"I wrote his wife not long ago of Red's illness," Ellen said, "but I didn't state all the facts; somehow I couldn't bring myself to do that. They are in London; they go over every winter. I had a card only yesterday from Charlotte giving a new address and promising to write soon."

"Wasn't he the man you told me of who had a bad nervous breakdown a few years ago? The one Red had stay with you here until he got back his nerve?"

"Yes; and he has been even a more brilliant operator ever since."

"I remember the whole story; there was a lot of thrill in it as you told it. How Red made him rest and build up and then fairly forced him to operate, against his will, to prove to him that he had got his nerve back? Jove! Do you think that man wouldn't cross the ocean in a hurry if he thought he could lift his finger to help our poor boy?"

King's speech had taken on such a fatherly tone of late that Ellen was not surprised to hear him thus allude to his senior.

"Yes, Jack Leaver would do anything for Red, but I know Red would never let us summon him from so far."

"Summon him from the antipodes—I would. And we don't have to consult Red. His wish is enough. Leave it to me, Mrs. Burns; I'll take all the responsibility."

She smiled at him, feeling that she must not express the very natural and unwelcome thought that to call a friend from so far away was to admit that the situation was desperate. Burns had said many times that Doctor Van Horn was using the very latest and most acceptable methods for his relief, and that his confidence in him was absolute. None the less she knew that the very sight of John Leaver's face would be like that of a shore light to a ship groping in a heavy fog.

Within twenty-four hours Jordan King came dashing in to wave a cable message before her. "Read that, and thank heaven that you have such friends in the world."

At a glance her eyes took in the pregnant line, and the first tears she had shed leaped to her eyes and misted them, so that she had to wipe them away to read the welcome words again.

We sail Saturday. Love to Doctor and Mrs. Burns.

LEAVER.

A week later, Burns, waking from an uneasy slumber, opened his eyes upon a new figure at his bedside. For a moment he stared uncomprehending into the dark, distinguished face of his old friend, then put out his uninjured hand with a weak clutch.

"Are you real, Jack?" he demanded in a whisper.

"As real as that bedpost. And mighty

glad to see you, my dear boy. They tell me the worst is over, and that you're improving. That's worth the journey to see."

"You didn't come from—England?"

"Of course I did. I'd come from the end of the world, and you know it! Why in the name of friendship didn't somebody send me word before?"

"Who sent it now?"

"That's a secret. I hoped to be able to do something for you, Red, just to even up the score a little, but the thing that's really been done has been by yourself. You put your own clean blood into this tussle and it's brought you through."

"I don't feel so very far through yet, but I suppose I'm not quite so much of a dead fish as I was a week ago. There's only one thing that bothers me."

"I can guess. Well, Red, I saw Doctor Van Horn on my way upstairs, and he tells me you're going to get a good hand out of this. He'll be up shortly to dress it, and then I may see for myself."

"That will be a comfort. I've wished a thousand times you might, though nobody could have given me better care than these bully fellows have. But I've a sort of superstition that one look at trouble from Jack Leaver is enough to make it cut and run."

By and by Dr. John Leaver came downstairs and joined his wife and Ellen. His face was grave with its habitual expression, but it lighted as the two looked up. "He's had about as rough a time as a man can and weather it," he said; "but I think the trouble is cornered at last, and there'll be no further outbreak. And the hand will come out better than could have been expected. He will be able to use it perfectly in time. But it will take him a good while to build up. He must have a sea voyage—a long one. That will do you all kinds of good, too," he added, his keen eyes on the face of his friend's wife.

"She looks etherealized," Charlotte Leaver said, studying Ellen affectionately. "You've had a long, anxious time, haven't you, Len, darling?" Mrs. Leaver went on. "And we knew nothing—we who care more than anybody in the world. You can't imagine how glad we are to be here now, even though we can't help a bit."

"You can help, you do. And I know what it means to Red to have his beloved friend come to him."

"Then I hope you know what it means to me to come," said John Leaver.

The Leavers stayed for several days, while Burns continued to improve, and before they left they had the pleasure of seeing him up and partially dressed, the bandages on his injured hand reduced in extent, and his eyes showing his release from torture. His face and figure gave touching evidence of what he had endured, but he promised them that before they saw him again he would be looking like himself.

"I wonder," Burns said, on the March day when he first came downstairs and dropped into his old favourite place in a corner of the big blue couch, "whether any other fellow was ever so pampered as I. I look like thirty cents, but I feel, in spite of this abominable limpness, as if my stock were worth a hundred cents on the dollar. And when we get back from the ocean trip I expect to be a regular fighting Fijian."

"You look better every day, dear," Ellen assured him. "And when it's all over, and you have done your first operation, you'll come home and say you were never so happy in your life."

Burns laughed. He looked over at Jordan King, who had come in on purpose to help celebrate the event of the appearance downstairs. "She promises me an operation as she would promise the Little-Un a sweetie, eh? Well, I can't say she isn't right. I was a bit tired when this thing began, but when I get my strength back I know how my little old 'lab' and machine shop will call to me. Just to-day I got an idea in my head that I believe will work out some day. My word, I know it will!"

The other two looked at each other, smiling joyously.

"He's getting well," said Ellen Burns.

"No doubt of it in the world," agreed Jordan King.

"Sit down here where I can look at you both," commanded the convalescent. "Jord, isn't my wife something to look at in that blue frock she's wearing? I like these things she melts into evenings, like that smoky blue she has on now. It seems to satisfy my eyes."

"Not much wonder in that. She would satisfy anybody's eyes."

"That's quite enough about me," Ellen declared. "The thing that's really interesting is that your eyes are brighter to-night, Red, than they have been for two long months. I believe it's getting downstairs."

"Of course it is. Downstairs has been a mythical sort of place for a good while. I couldn't quite believe in it. I've thought a thousand times of this blue couch and these pillows. I've thought of that old grand piano of yours, and of how it would seem to hear you play it again. Play for me now, will you, Len?"

She sat down in her old place, and his eyes watched her hungrily, as King could plainly see. To the younger man the love between these two was something to study and believe in, something to hope for as a wonderful possibility in his own case.

When Ellen stopped playing Burns spoke musingly. Speech seemed a necessity for him to-night—happiness overflowed and must find expression.

"I've had a lot of stock advice for my patients that'll mean something I understand for myself now," he said. He sat almost upright among the blue pillows, his arm outstretched along the back of the couch, his long legs comfortably extended. It was no longer the attitude of the invalid but of the well man enjoying earned repose. "I wonder how often I've said to some tired mother or too-busy housewife who longed for rest: 'If you were to become crippled or even forbidden to work any more and made to rest for good, how happy these past years would seem to you when you were tired because you had accomplished something.' I can say that now with personal conviction of its truth. It looks to me as if to come in dog-tired and drop into this corner with the memory of a good job done would be the best fun I've ever had."

"I know," King nodded. "I learned that, too, last spring."

"Of course you did. And now, instead of going to work, I've got to take this blamed sea voyage of a month. Van and Leaver are pretty hard on me, don't you think? The consolation in that, though, is that my wife needs it quite as much as I do. I want to tan those cheeks of hers. Len, will you wear the brown tweeds on shipboard?"

"Of course I will. How your mind seems to run to clothes to-night. What will Your Highness wear himself?"

"The worst old clothes I can find. Then when I get back I'll go to the tailor's and start life all over again, with the neatest lot of stuff he can make me—a regular honeymoon effect." Burns laughed, lifting his chin with the old look of purpose and power touching his thin face.

"I'm happy to-night," he went on; "there's no use denying it. I'm not sorry, now it's over, I've had this experience, for I've learned some things I've never known before and wouldn't have found out any other way. I know now what it means to be down where life doesn't seem worth much, and how it feels to have the other fellow trying to pull you out. I know how the whisper of a voice you love sounds to you in the middle of a black night, when you think you can't bear another minute of pain. Oh, I know a lot of things I can't talk about, but they'll make a difference in the future. If I don't have more patience with my patients it'll be because memory is a treacherous thing, and I've forgotten what I have no business to forget—because the good Lord means me to remember!"

CHAPTER XVI

White Lilacs Again

It was the first day of May. Burns and Ellen had not been at home two days after their return from the long, slow sea voyage which had done wonders for them both, when Burns received a long-distance message which sent him to his wife with his eyes sparkling in the old way.

"Great luck, Len!" he announced. "I'm to get my first try-out in operating, after the late unpleasantness, on an out-of-town case. Off in an hour with Amy for a place two hundred miles away in a spot I never heard of—promises to be interesting. Anyhow, I feel like a small boy with his first kite, likely to go straight off the ground hitched to the tail of it."

"I'm glad for you, Red. And I wish"—she bit her lip and turned away—"it may be a wonderful case."

"That's not what you started to say." He came close, laid a hand on either side of her face, and turned it up so that he could look into it, his lips smiling. "Tell me. I'll wager I know what you wish."

"No, you can't."

"That you could go with me—to take Amy's place and assist."

A flood of colour poured over her face, such a telltale, significant colour as he had rarely seen there before. She would have concealed it from him, but he was merciless. A strange, happy look came into his own face. "Len, don't hide that from me. It's the one thing I've always wished you'd show, and you never have. I'm such a jealous beggar myself I've wanted you to care—that way, and I've never been able to discover a trace of it."

"But I'm not really jealous in the way you think. How could I be?—with not the slightest cause. It's only—envy of Amy because she is—so necessary to you. O Red, I never, never meant to say it!"

"I'd rather hear you say it than anything else on earth. I'd like to hear you own that you were mad with jealousy, because I've been eaten up with it myself ever since I first laid eyes on you. Not that you've ever given me a reason for it, but because it's my red-headed nature. Now I must go; but I'll take your face with me, my Len, and if I do a good piece of work it'll be for love of you."

"And of your work, Red. I'm not jealous of that; I'm too proud of it."

"I know you are, bless you."

Then he was off, all his old vigour showing in his preparations for the hurried trip, and as he went away Ellen felt as might those on shore watching a lusty life-saver put off in a boat to pull for a sinking ship.

Burns and Amy Mathewson were away three days, during which Red kept Ellen even more closely in touch with himself than usual, by means of the long wire. When he returned it was with the bearing of a conqueror, for the case had tried his regained mettle and he had triumphed more surely than he could have hoped.

"The hand's as good as new, Len, and the touch not a particle affected. Van's a trump, and I stopped on the way out to tell him so. He was pleased as a boy; think of it, Len—my ancient enemy and my new good friend! And the case is fine as silk. They've a good local man to look after it till I come again, which will be Thursday. And I'm going to drive there—and take you—and Jord King and Jord's mother. How's that for a plan?"

"It sounds very jolly, Red, but will the Kings go? And why Mrs. King? Will she care to?"

"Because I've found some old friends of hers in the place, though I'll not tell her whom. Besides, I want to keep on her right side, for reasons. And Jord's back has been bothering him lately and I've prescribed a rest. We'll take the Kings' limousine and go in state. It'll be arranged in five minutes, see if it won't. By the way, Jord says Aleck's new arm is really going to do him some service besides improving his looks."

He pulled her away to the telephone and held her on his knee while he talked to Jordan King, giving her a laughing hug, when, to judge by the things he was saying into the transmitter, he had brought about his effect.

"Yes, I know I sound crazy," he admitted to King, "but you must give something to a man who has been buried alive and dug up again. I've taken this notion and I'm going to carry it through. Mrs. King will enjoy every foot of the way, and you and I will jump out and pick apple blossoms for the ladies whenever they ask. It's a peach of a plan, and the whole idea is to minister to my pride. I want to arrive in a great prince of a car like yours and impress the natives down there. See? Yes, go and put it up to your mother, and then call me up. Don't you dare say no!"

"No wonder he's astonished," Ellen commented while they waited. "For you, who are never content except when you're at the steering wheel, to ask Jordan, who is another just like you, to elect to travel in a limousine with a liveried chauffeur—well, I admit I am puzzled myself."

"Why, it's simple enough. I want to take you and Mrs. Alexander King. She wouldn't go a step in Jord's roadster at his pace. And if she would, and we went in pairs, Jord would be always wanting to change off and take you with him—and as you very well know I'm not made that way. Stop guessing, Len, and prepare yourself to break down Mrs. King's opposition, if she makes any—which I don't expect."

Mrs. King made no opposition, or none which her son thought best to convey to the Burnses, and the trip was arranged.

"Is there a good hotel in the place?" Ellen asked.

"No hotel within miles—nor anything else. We're to stay overnight with the family. You won't mind. They can put us up pretty comfortably, even if not just as we're accustomed to be." Burns's eyes were twinkling, and he refused to say more on the subject.

It did not matter. It was early May, and the world was a wilderness of budding life, and to go motoring seemed the finest way possible to get into sympathy with spring at her loveliest. And although Ellen would have much preferred to drive alone with her husband in his own car, she found herself anticipating the affair, as it was now arranged, with not a little curiosity to stimulate her interest. Mrs. Alexander King, for her son's sake, was sure to be a complaisant and agreeable companion, and Ellen was glad to feel that such a pleasure might come her way.

"This is great stuff!" exulted Jordan King early on Thursday morning as the big, shining car, standing before Burns's door, received its full complement of passengers. "Mother and I are tremendously honoured, aren't we, mother?"

"Even though we had the audacity to invite ourselves and ask for this magnificent car?" Burns inquired, grasping Mrs. Alexander King's gloved hand, and smiling at her as her delicate face was lifted to him with a look of really charming greeting. He knew well enough that she liked him in spite of certain pretty plain words he had said to her in the past, and he had prepared himself to make her like him still better on this journey together. "I'm the one who is responsible, you know. I've merely broken out in a new place."

"We appreciate your caring to include us in your party," Mrs. King said cordially. "The car is all too little used, for Jordan prefers his own, and I go about mostly in the small coupe. I have never taken so long a drive as you plan, and it will doubtless be a pleasant experience. I see so little of my son I am happy to be with him on such a trip."

"Altogether we're mightily pleased with the whole arrangement," declared Jordan King, regarding Mrs. Burns with high approval. "Mother, did you ever see a more distinguished-looking pair?"

"In spite of our brown faces?" Ellen challenged him gayly.

"My wife's face simply turns peachy when she tans. I look like an Indian," observed Burns, bestowing certain professional luggage where it would be most out of the way.

"That's it; you've said it. Great Indian Chief go make big medicine for sick squaw; take along whole wigwam; wigwam tickled to death to go!" And King settled himself with an air of complete satisfaction.

He had had no word from Anne Linton for nearly two months, and was as restless as a young man may well be when his affairs do not go to please him. She had kept her promise and had written from time to time, but though her letters were the most interesting human documents King had ever dreamed a woman could write, they were, from the point of view of the suitor, extremely unsatisfying. As she had agreed, she had given him with each letter an address to which he might send an immediate reply, and he had made the most of each such opportunity; but, since it takes two to seal a bargain, he had not been able to feel his cause much advanced by all his efforts. He had welcomed this chance to accompany Burns as a diversion from his restless thoughts, for a few days' interval in his engineering plans, caused by a delay in the arrival of certain necessary material, was making him wild with eagerness for something—anything—to happen.

Two hundred miles in a high-powered

car over finely macadamized roads are more quickly and comfortably covered in these days than a thirty-mile drive behind horses over such country highways as existed a decade ago. Aleck, at the wheel, his master's orders in his willing ears from time to time, gradually accelerated his rate of speed until by the end of the first two hours he was carrying his party along at a pace which Mrs. King had frequently condemned as one which would be to her unbearable. Burns and King exchanged glances more than once as the car flew past other travellers, and the good lady, talking happily with Ellen or absorbed in some far-reaching view, took no note of the fact that she was annihilating space with a smooth swiftness comparable only to the flight of some big, strong-winged bird.

"Over halfway there, and plenty of time for lunch," Burns announced. "And here's the best roadside inn in the country. If it hadn't been for our coming this way I should have suggested bringing our own hampers, but I wanted you to have some of this little Englishman's brook trout and hot scones."

Mrs. King enjoyed that hot and delicious meal as she had seldom enjoyed a luncheon anywhere. As she sat at the faultlessly served table, her eyes travelling from the wide view at the window to the faces of her companions, she grew more and more cheerful in manner, and was even heard to laugh softly aloud now and then at one of Burns's gay quips, turning to Ellen in appreciation of her husband's wit, or to Jordan himself as he came back at his friend with a rejoinder worth hearing.

"This is doing my mother a world of good," King said in Ellen's ear as the party came out on a wide porch to rest for a half hour before taking to the car again. "I don't know when I've seen her expand like this and seem really to be forgetting her cares and sorrows."

"It's a pleasure to watch her," Ellen agreed. "Red vowed this morning that he meant to bring about that very thing, and he's succeeding much better than I had dared to hope."

"Who wouldn't be jolly in a party where

Red was one? Did you ever see the dear fellow so absolutely irresistible? Sometimes I think there's a bit of hypnotism about Red, he gets us all so completely."

"What are you two whispering about?" said a voice behind them, and they turned to look into the brilliant hazel eyes both were thinking of at the moment.

"You," King answered promptly.

"Rebelling against the autocracy of the Indian Chief?"

"No. Prostrating ourselves before his bulky form. He's some Indian to-day."

"He will be before the day is over, I promise you. He'll call a council around the campfire to-night, and plenty pipes will be smoked. Everybody do as Big Chief says, eh?"

"Sure thing, Geronimo; that's what we came for."

"You don't know what you came for. Absolutely preposterous this thing is—surgeon going to visit his case and bringing along a lot of people who don't know a mononuclear leucocyte from an eosinophile cell."

"Do you know a vortex filament from a diametral plane?" demanded King.

Burns laughed. "Come, let's be off! I must spare half an hour to show Mrs. King a certain view somewhat off the main line."

The afternoon was gone before they could have believed it, detours though there were several, as there usually are in a road-mending season. As the car emerged from a long run through wooded country and passed a certain landmark carefully watched for by Red Pepper, he spoke to Aleck.

"Run slowly now, please. And be ready to turn to the left at a point that doesn't show much beforehand."

They were proceeding through somewhat sparsely settled country, though marked here and there by comfortable farmhouses of a more than ordinarily attractive type—apparently homes of prosperous people with an eye to appearances. Then quite suddenly the car, rounding a turn, came into a different region, one of cultivated wildness, of studied effects so cleverly disguised that they would seem to the unobservant only the efforts of nature at her best. A long, heavily shaded avenue of oaks, with high, untrimmed hedges of shrubbery on each side, curved enticingly before them, and all at once, Burns, looking sharply ahead, called, "There, by that big pine, Aleck—to the left." In a minute more the car turned in at a point where a rough stone gateway marked the entrance to nothing more extraordinary than a pleasant wood.

"Patient lives in a hut in the forest?" King inquired with interest. "Or a rich man's hunting lodge?"

"You'll soon see." Burns's eyes were ahead; a slight smile touched his lips.

The car swept around curve after curve of the wood, came out upon the shore of a small lake and, skirting it halfway round, plunged into a grove of pines. Then, quite without warning, there showed beyond the pines a long, white-plumed row of small trees of a sort unmistakable—in May. Beside the row lay a garden, gay with all manner of spring flowers, and farther, through the trees, began to gleam the long, low outlines of a great house.

"Stop just here, Aleck, for a minute," Burns requested, and the car came to a standstill. Burns looked at Jordan King.

"Ever see that row of white lilacs before, Jord?" he asked with interest.

King was staring at it, a strange expression of mingled perplexity and astonishment upon his fine, dark face. After a minute he turned to Burns.

"What—when—where—" he stammered, and stopped, gazing again at the lilac hedge and the box-bordered beds with their splashes of bright colour.

"Well, I don't know what, when, or where, if you don't," Burns returned.

But evidently King did know, or it came to him at that instant, for he set his lips in a certain peculiar way which his friend understood meant an attempt at quick disguise of strong feeling. He gave his mother one glance and sat back in his seat. Then he looked again at Burns.

"What is this, anyway?" he asked rather sternly. "The home of your patient, or a show place you've stopped to let us look at?"

"My patient's in the house up there. Drive on, Aleck, please. They'll be expecting us at the back of the house, where the long porches are, and where they're probably having afternoon tea at this minute." He glanced at his watch. "Happy time to arrive, isn't it?"

Ellen found herself experiencing a most extraordinary sensation of excitement as the car rounded the drive and approached the porch, where she could see a number of people gathered. The place was not more imposing than many with which she was familiar, and if it had been the home of one of the world's greatest there would have been nothing disconcerting to her in the prospect. But something in her husband's manner assured her that he had been preparing a surprise for them all, and she had no means of guessing what it might be. The little hasty sketch of lilac trees against a spring sky, though she had seen it, had naturally made no such impression upon her as upon King, and she did not even recall it now.

The car rolled quietly up to the porch steps, and immediately a tall figure sprang down them. "It's Gardner Coolidge, my old college friend, Len," Burns said in his wife's ear. "Remember him?" The afternoon sunlight shone upon the smooth, dark hair and thin, aristocratic face of a man who spoke eagerly, his quick glance sweeping the occupants of the car.

"Mrs. King! This is a great pleasure, I assure you—a great pleasure. Mrs. Burns—we are delighted. And this is your son, Mrs. King—welcome to you, my dear sir! Red, no need to say we're glad to see you back. Let me help you, Mrs. King. Don't tell me you wouldn't have known me; that would be a blow. Alicia"—he turned to the graceful figure approaching across the porch to meet the elder lady of the party as she came up the steps upon the arm of the man who had taken her from the car—"Mrs. King, this is my wife."

Red Pepper Burns, laughing and shaking hands warmly with Alicia Coolidge, was watching Mrs. Alexander King as, after the first look of bewilderment, she cried out softly with pleasure at recognizing the son of an old friend.

"But it has all been kept secret from me," she was saying. "I had no possible idea of where we were coming, and I am sure my son had not." She turned to that son, but she could not get his attention, for the reason that his astonished gaze was fastened upon a person who had at that moment appeared in the doorway and paused there.

CHAPTER XVII

Red's Dearest Patients

Jordan King looked, and looked again, and it was a wonder he did not rub his eyes to make sure he was fully awake. As he looked the figure in the doorway came forward. It was that of a girl in a white serge coat and skirt, with a smart little white hat upon her richly ruddy hair, and the look, from head to foot, of one who had just returned to a place where she belonged. And the next instant Anne Linton was greeting Ellen Burns and coming up to be presented to Mrs. Alexander King.

"This is my little sister, Mrs. King," said Gardner Coolidge, smiling, and putting his arm about the white-serge-clad shoulders. "She is your hostess, you know. Alicia and I are only making her a visit."

"I am so glad you are here, Mrs. King," said a voice Jordan King well remembered, and Anne Linton's eyes looked straight into those of her oldest guest, whose own were puzzled.

"I think," said Mrs. King, holding the firm young hand which she had taken, "I have seen you before, my dear, though my memory—"

"Yes, Mrs. King," the girl replied—and there was not the smallest shadow of triumph discernible in her tone or look—"you have. I came to see your son in the hospital, with Mrs. Burns, just before I left. It's not strange you have forgotten me, for we went away almost at once. We are so delighted to have you come to see us. Isn't it delightful that you knew our mother so well at school?"

Well, it came Jordan King's turn in the end, although Anne Linton, so extraordinarily labelled "hostess" by her brother, discharged every duty of greeting her other guests before she turned to him. Meanwhile he had stood, frankly staring, hat in hand and growing colour on his cheek, while his eyes seemed to grow darker and darker under his heavily marked brows. When Anne turned to him he had no words for her, and hardly a smile, though his good breeding came to his rescue and put him through the customary forms of action, dazed though he yet was. He found himself presented to other people on the porch, whom he recognized as undoubtedly those whom he had met in the passing car at the time when he was in doubt as to Anne's identity. Her aunt, uncle, and cousins they proved to be, though the young man whom he remembered as being present on that occasion was now happily absent. Jordan King found himself completely reconciled to this at once.

"How is our patient?" Burns said to Anne at the first opportunity. "Shall I go up at once?"

"Oh, please wait a minute, Doctor Burns; I want to go with you, and I must see my guests having some tea first."

There followed, for King, what seemed an interminable interval of time, during which he was forced to sit beside one of Anne's girl cousins—and a very pretty girl she was, too, only he didn't seem able to appreciate it—drinking tea, and handing sugar, and doing all the proper things. In the midst of this Anne vanished with Red Pepper at her heels, leaving the tea table to Mrs. Coolidge. At this point, however,

King found himself glad to listen to Miss Stockton.

"I don't suppose anybody in the world but Anne Linton Coolidge would have thought of sending two hundred miles for a surgeon to operate on her housekeeper," she was saying when his attention was arrested by her words. "But she thinks such a lot of Timmy—Mrs. Timmins—she would pay any sum to keep her in the world. She was Anne's nurse, you see, and of course Anne is fond of her. And I'm sure we're glad she did send for him, for it gave us the pleasure of meeting Doctor Burns, and of course we understand now why she thought nobody else in the world could pull Timmy through. He's such an interesting personality, don't you think so? We're all crazy about him."

"Oh, yes, everybody's crazy about him," King admitted readily. "And certainly two hundred miles isn't far to send for a surgeon these days."

"Of course not—only I don't suppose it's done every day for one's housekeeper, do you? But nobody ever knows what Anne's going to do—least of all now, when she's just back, after the most extraordinary performance." She stopped, looking at him curiously. "I suppose you know all about it—much more than we, in fact, since you met her when she was in that hospital. Did you ever hear of a rich girl's doing such a thing anyway? Going off to sell books for a whole year just because"—she stopped again, and bit her lip, then went on quickly: "Everybody knows about it, and you would be sure to hear it sooner or later. Doctor Burns knows, anyhow, and—"

"Please don't tell me anything I oughtn't to hear," Jordan's sense of honour impelled him to say. He recognized the feminine type before him, and though he longed to know all about everything he did not want to know it in any way Anne would not like.

But there was no stopping the fluffy-haired young person. "Really, everybody knows; the countryside fairly rang with it a year ago. You might even have read it in the papers, only you wouldn't remember. A girl book agent killed herself in Anne's house here because

Anne wouldn't buy her book. Did you ever hear of anything so absurd as Anne's thinking it was her fault? Of course the girl was insane, and Anne had absolutely nothing to do with it. And then Anne took the girl's book and went off to sell it herself—and find out, she said, how such things could happen. I don't know whether she found out." Miss Stockton laughed very charmingly. "All I know is we're tremendously thankful to have her back. Nothing's the same with her away. We don't know if she'll stay, though. Nobody can tell about Anne, ever."

"Is this your home, too?" King managed to ask. His brain was whirling with the shock of this astonishing revelation. He wanted to get off by himself and think about it.

"Oh, no, indeed, no such luck. We live across the lake in a much less beautiful place, only of course we're here a great deal when Anne's home. My mother would be a mother to Anne if Anne would let her, but she's the most independent creature—prefers to live here with just Timmy and old Campbell, the butler who's been with the family since time began. Timmy's more than a housekeeper, of course. Anne's made almost a real chaperon out of her, and she is very dignified and nice."

King would have had the entire family history, he was sure, if a diversion had not occurred in the nature of a general move to show the guests to their rooms, with the appearance of servants, and the removal of luggage. In his room presently, therefore, King had a chance to get his thoughts together. One thing was becoming momentarily clear to him: his being here was with Anne's permission—and she was willing to see him; she had kept her promise. As for all the rest, he didn't care much. And when he thought of the moment during which his mother had looked so kindly into Anne's eyes, not recognizing her, he laughed aloud. Let Mrs. King retreat from that position now if she wanted to. As for himself, he was not at all sure that he cared a straw to have it thus so clearly proved that Anne was what she had seemed to be. Had he not known it all along? His heart sang with the thought that he had been ready to marry her, no matter what her position in the world.

And now he wondered how many hours it would be before he should have his chance to see her alone, if for but five minutes. Well, at least he could look at her. And that, as he descended the stairs with the others, he found well worth doing. Anne and Gardner Coolidge were meeting them at the foot, and the young hostess had changed her white outing garb for a most enchanting other white, which showed her round arms through soft net and lace and made her yet a new type of girl in King's thought of her.

She had a perfectly straightforward way of meeting his eyes, though her own were bewildering even so, without any coquetry in her use of them. She was not blushing and shy, she was self-possessed and radiant. King could understand, as he looked at her now, how she had felt over that affair of the tragedy suddenly precipitated into her life, and what strength of character it must have taken to send her out from this secluded and perfect home into a rough world, that she might find out for herself "how such things could happen." And as he watched her, playing hostess in this home of hers, looking after everybody's comfort with that ease and charm which proclaims a lifetime of previous training and custom, his heart grew fuller and fuller of pride and love and longing.

The dinner hour passed, a merry hour at a dignified table, served by the old butler who made a rite of his service, his face never relaxing though the laughter rang never so contagiously. Burns and Coolidge were the life of the company, the latter seeming a different man from the one who had come to consult his old chum as to the trouble in his life. Mrs. Coolidge, quiet and very attractive in her reserved, fair beauty, made an interesting foil to Ellen Burns, and the two, beside the rather fussy aunt and cousins, seemed to belong together.

"Anne, we must show Doctor Burns our plans for the cottage," Coolidge said to his sister as they left the table. He turned to Ellen, walking beside her. "She's almost persuaded us to build on a corner of her own estate—at least a summer place, for a starter. You know Red prescribed for us a cottage, and we haven't yet carried out his prescription But this sister of mine, since she met him, has acquired the idea that any prescription of his simply has to be filled, and she won't let Alicia and me alone till we've done this thing. Shall we all walk along down there? There'll be just about time before dark for you to see the site, and the plans shall come later."

The whole party trooped down the steps into the garden. King was a clever engineer, but he could not do any engineering which seemed to count in this affair. Never seeming to avoid him, Anne was never where he could get three words alone with her. She devoted herself to his mother, to Ellen, or to Burns himself, and none of these people gave him any help. Not that he wanted them to. He bided his time, and meanwhile he took some pleasure in showing his lady that he, too, could play his part until it should suit her to give him his chance.

But when, as the evening wore on, it began to look as if she were deliberately trying to prevent any interview whatever, he grew unhappy. And at last, the party having returned to the house and gathered in a delightful old drawing-room, he took his fate in his hands. At a moment when Anne stood beside Red Pepper looking over some photographs lying on the grand piano, he came up behind them.

"Miss Coolidge," he said, "I wonder if you would show me that lilac hedge by moonlight."

"I'm afraid there isn't any moon," she answered with a merry, straightforward look. "It will be as dark as a pocket down by that hedge, Mr. King. But I'll gladly show it to you to-morrow morning—as early as you like. I'm a very early riser."

"As early as six o'clock?" he asked eagerly.

She nodded. "As early as that. It is a perfect time on a May morning."

"And you won't go anywhere now?"

"How can I?" she parried, smiling. "These are my guests."

Burns glanced at his friend, his hazel eyes full of suppressed laughter. "Better be contented with that, old fellow. That row of lilacs will be very nice at six o'clock to-morrow morning. Mayn't I come, too, Miss Coolidge?"

"Of course you may." Her sparkling glance met his. Evidently they were very good friends, and understood each other.

"If he does," said King, in a sort of growl, "he'll have something to settle with me."

He went to bed in a peculiar frame of mind. Why had she wanted to waste all these hours when at nine in the morning the party was to leave for its return trip? Well, he supposed morning would come sometime, though it seemed, at midnight, a long way off.

"Want me to call you at five-thirty, Jord?" Burns had inquired of him at parting.

"No, thanks," he had replied. "I'll not miss it."

"A fellow might lie awake so long thinking about it that he'd go off into a sound sleep just before daylight, and sleep right through his early morning appointment," urged his loyal friend. "Better let me—"

"Oh, you go on to bed!" requested King irritably.

"No gratitude to one who has brought all this to pass, eh?"

"Heaps of it. But this evening has been rather a facer."

"Not at all. There were a dozen times when you might have rushed in and got a little quiet place all to yourself, with only the stars looking on. Plenty of openings."

"I didn't see 'em. You were always in the way."

"I was! Well, I like that. Had to be ordinarily attentive to my hostess, hadn't I? It wasn't for me to take shy little boys by the hand and lead them up to the little girls they fancied."

"I don't want to be led up by the hand,

thank you. Good-night!"

King was up at daybreak, which in May comes reasonably early. Stealing down through the quiet house, the windows of which seemed to be all wide open to the morning air, he came out upon the porch and took the path to the lilac hedge. Arrived there at only twenty minutes before the appointed hour, he had so long a wait that he began to grow both impatient and chagrined. At quarter-past six he was feeling very much like stalking back to the house and retiring to his room, when the low sound of a motor arrested him, and he wheeled, to discover a long, low, gray car, of a type with which he was not familiar, sailing gracefully around the long curve of the driveway toward him. A trim figure in gray, with a small gray velvet hat pulled close over auburn hair, was at the wheel, and a vivid face was smiling at him. But the air of the driver as she drew up beside him was not at all sentimental, rather it was businesslike.

"I'm awfully sorry to be late," she said, "but I couldn't possibly help it. I got up at four, to make a call I had to make and be back, but I was detained. And even now I must be off again, without any lingering by lilac hedges. What shall we do about it?"

"I'll go with you." And King stepped into the car.

"With or without an invitation?" Her eyes were laughing, though her lips had sobered.

"With or without. And you know you came back for me."

"I came back for a basket of things I must get from the house. Also, of course, to explain my detention."

"Out selling books, I suppose?" he questioned, not caring much what he said, now that he had her to himself. "You must make a great impression as a book agent. If only you had tried that way in our town. And I—I took you in my car under the pleasant impression that I was giving you a treat—on that first trip, you know. By the second trip I had acquired a sneaking suspicion that motoring wasn't such a novelty to you as I had at first supposed."

They had flown around the remaining curves and were at a rear door of the house. Anne jumped out, was gone for ten minutes or so, and emerged with a servant following with a great hamper. This was bestowed at King's feet, and the car was off again, Anne driving with the ease of a veteran.

"You see," she explained, "late last evening I had news of the serious illness of a girl friend of mine. I went to see her, but after I came back I couldn't be easy about her, and so I got up quite early this morning and went again. She was much better, precisely as Doctor Burns had assured me she would be. By and by perhaps I shall learn to trust him as absolutely as all the rest of you do."

"Burns! You don't mean to say you had him out to see a case last night—after—"

She nodded, and her profile, under the snug gray hat, was a little like that of a handsome and somewhat mischievous but strong-willed boy. "Was that so dreadful of me—as a hostess? I admit that a doctor ought to be allowed to rest when he is away from home, but I knew that he was just back from a long voyage and was feeling fit as a fiddle, as he himself said. And there is really no very competent man in the town where my friend is ill; it was such a wonderful chance for her to have great skill at her service. And such skill! Oh, how he went to work for her! It made one feel at once that something was being done, where before people had merely tried to do things."

King was making rapid calculation. At the end of it, "Would you mind telling me whether you have had any sleep at all?" he begged.

She turned her face toward him for an instant. "Do I look so haggard and wan?" she queried with a quick glance. "Yes, I had a good two hours. And I'm so happy now to know that Estelle is sleeping quietly that it's much better than to have slept myself."

"Do you do this sort of thing often?"

"Not just such spectacular night work, but I do try to see that a little is done to look after a few people who have had a terribly hard time of it. But this is all—or mostly—since I came back from my year away. I learned just a few things during that year, you know."

"Your cousin—do you mind?—gave me just a bit of an idea why you went," he ventured.

"Oh, Leila Stockton." Her lips took on an amused curl. "Of course Leila would. She—chatters. But she's a dear girl; it's just that she can't easily get a new point of view."

He pressed her with his questions, for his discernment told him that it was of no use, while they were flying along the road at this pace, with a hamper at their feet—or at his feet, crowding him rather uncomfortably and forcing him to sit with cramped legs—no use for him to talk of the subject uppermost in his anxious mind. So he got from her, as well as he could, the story of the year, and presently had her telling him eagerly of the people she had met, and the progress she had made in the study of human beings. It was really an engrossing tale, quietly as she told it, and many as were the details he saw that she kept back.

"I found out one thing very early," she said. "I knew that I could never come back and live as I had lived before, with no thought of any one but myself."

"I don't believe you had ever done that."

"I had—I had, if ever any one did. I went away to school in Paris for two years; I wouldn't go to college—how I wish I had! I was the gayest, most thoughtless girl you ever knew until—the thing happened that sent my world spinning upside down. Why, Mr. King, I was so selfish and so thoughtless that I could turn that poor girl away from my door with a careless denial, and never see that she was desperate—that it wanted only one more such turning away to make her do the thing she did."

He saw her press her lips together, her eyes fixed on the road ahead, and he saw the beautiful brows contract, as if the memory still were too keen for her to bear calmly.

"You have certainly atoned a hundred times over," he said gently, "for any carelessness in the past. How could you know how she was feeling? And she was insane, Miss Stockton said."

"No more insane than I am now—simply desperate with weariness and failure. And I should have seen; I did see. I just—didn't care. I was busy trying on a box of new frocks from a French dressmaker, frocks of silk and lace—of silk and lace, Jordan King, while she hadn't clothes enough to keep her warm! And I couldn't spare the time to look at the girl's book! Well, I learned what it was to have people turn me from their doors—I, with plenty of money at my command, no matter how I elected to dress cheaply and go to cheap boarding places, and—insist on cheap beds at hospitals." Her tone was full of scorn. "After all, did I ever really suffer anything of what she suffered? Never, for always I knew that at any minute I could turn from a poor girl into a rich one, throw my book in the faces of those who refused to buy it, and telephone my anxious family. They did come on and try to get me away—once. I went with them—for the day. It was the day you met me. And always there was the interest of the adventure. It was an adventure, you know, a big one."

"I should say it was. And when you were at the hospital—"

"Accepting expensive rooms and free medical attendance—oh, wasn't I a fraud? How I felt it I can never tell you. But I could—and did—send back Doctor Burns a draft in part payment, though I thought he would never imagine where it came from. He did, though. What do you suppose he told me last night when we were driving home?—this morning it was, of course."

"I can't guess," King admitted, suffering a distinct and poignant pang of jealousy at thought of Red Pepper Burns driving through the night with this girl, on an errand of mercy though it had been.

"He told me," she said slowly, "that he learned all about me while I was in the hospital. One night, when I was at the worst, he sent Miss Arden out for a rest and sat beside me himself. And in my foolish, delirious wanderings I gave him the whole story, or enough of it so that he pieced out the rest. And he never told a soul, not even his wife; wasn't that wonderful of him? And treated me exactly the same as if he didn't practically know I wasn't what I seemed. You see, I wasn't far enough away from that poor girl's suicide, when I was so ill last year, but that it was always in my mind. Even yet I dream of it at times."

They were entering a large manufacturing town, the streets in the early morning full of factory operatives on their way to work, dinner-pails in hands and shawls over heads. Anne drove carefully, often throwing a smile at a group of children or slowing down more than the law decreed to avoid making some weary-faced woman hurry. And when at length she drew up before a dingy brick tenement house, of a type the most unpromising, King discovered that her "friend" was one of these very people.

He carried the hamper up two flights of ramshackle stairs and set it inside the door she indicated. Then he unwillingly withdrew to the car, where he sat waiting—and wondering. It was not long he had to wait, in point of time, but his impatience was growing upon him. All this was very well, and threw interesting lights upon a girl's character, but—it would be nine o'clock all too soon. To be sure, though Red Pepper bore him away, he knew the road back—he could come back as soon as he pleased, with nobody to set hours of departure for him. But he did not mean to go away this first time without the thing he wanted, if it was to be his.

She came running downstairs, face aglow with relief and pleasure, and sent the car smoothly away. And now it was that King discovered how a girl may fence and parry, so that a man may not successfully introduce the subject he is burning to speak of, without riding roughshod over her objection. And presently he gave it up, biding his time. He sat silent while she talked, and then finally, when she too grew silent, he let the minutes slip by without another word. Thus it was that they drew up at the house, still speechless concerning the great issue between them.

It was only a little past seven; nobody was in sight except a maid servant, who slipped discreetly away. King took one look into a small room at the right of the hall, a sort of small den or office it seemed to be. Then he turned to Anne and put out his hand. "Will you come in here, please?" he requested.

She looked at him for a moment without giving him her hand, then preceded him into the room. There was a heavy curtain of dull blue silk hanging by the door frame, and King noiselessly drew this across. Then he turned and confronted the girl. She had drawn off her motoring gloves, but made no motion to remove either the rough gray coat in which she had been driving or the small gray velvet hat drawn smoothly down over her curls with a clever air of its own. Altogether she looked not in the least like a hostess, but very like a traveller who has only paused for a brief stop on a journey to be immediately continued.

He stood there watching her for a minute, himself a challenging figure with his dark, bright face, his fine young height, his air of—quite suddenly—commanding the situation. And he was between the girl and the door. The two pairs of eyes looked straight into each other.

"Well?" he said.

"Well?" said Anne Linton Coolidge in return.

"Did you expect me to wait any longer?"

"I was afraid you might come and go—and never say so much as 'Well?'" said she.

This was more than mortal man could bear—and there was no more waiting done by anybody. When Jordan King had—temporarily—done satisfying the hunger of his lips and arms, he spoke again, looking down searchingly at a face into which he had brought plenty of splendid colour.

"If I had found you in that poor place I thought I should, it would have been just the same," he said.

"I really believe it would," admitted Anne.

Half an hour afterward, emerging from the small room which had held such a big experience, the pair discovered Red Pepper Burns just descending the stairway. He scrutinized their faces sharply, then advanced upon them. They met him halfway. He gravely took

Anne's hand and set his fingers on her pulse.

"Too rapid," he said with a shake of the head. "Altogether too rapid. You have been undergoing much excitement—and so early in the morning, too. As your physician I must caution you against such untimely hours."

He felt of King's wrist, and again he shook his head. "Worse and worse," he announced. "Not only rapid, but bounding. The heart is plainly overworked. These cases are contagious. One acts upon the other—no doubt of it—no doubt at all. I would suggest—"

He found both his arms grasped by Jordan King's strong hands, and he allowed himself to be held tightly by that happy young man. "Give us your best wishes!" demanded his captor.

"Why, you've had those from the first. I saw this coming before either of you," Burns replied.

"Not before I did," asserted King.

"Not before I did," declared Anne.

Then the two looked at each other, and Burns, smiling at them, his hazel eyes very bright, requested to be restored the use of his arms. This being conceded, he laid those arms about the shoulders before him and drew the two young people close within them.

"You two are the most satisfactory and the dearest patients I've ever had," declared Red Pepper Burns.

THE END.

Printed in the United Kingdom
by Lightning Source UK Ltd.
135001UK00001B/447/A

9 788184 564327